I0520892

Men Can Do Romance

A Novella

Michael Holloway Perronne

CHANCES PRESS
www.chancespress.com

Men Can Do Romance

Copyright © 2013 by Michael Holloway Perronne

All rights reserved. Without limiting the rights under copyright reserved above, no part of this publication may be reproduced, stored in or introduced into a retrieval system, or transmitted, in any form, or by any means (electronic, mechanical, photocopying, recording, or otherwise) without the prior written permission of both the copyright owner and the above publisher of this book.

This is a work of fiction. Names, characters, places, brands, media, and incidents are either the product of the author's imagination or are used fictitiously. The author acknowledges the trademarked status and trademark owners of various products referenced in this work of fiction, which have been used without permission. The publication/use of these trademarks is not authorized, associated with, or sponsored by the trademark owners.

ISBN: 9780615885650

Published by Chances Press, LLC

www.chancespress.com

Chapter One- Elliot

Professional that quantifies risk.

That's how I describe my job when someone asks, "Elliot, what the hell is an actuary anyway?" Sure, I could go into all the nitty gritty details about health care laws I have to memorize and complex mathematical equations I have to solve. But those four words really summarize it. I tell a health insurance company how much they should charge you and if you're even worth the risk. All day long I decide if whatever is worth taking a chance. I have to look at things within a black and white world. There can be no gray. So how could that not bleed over into my personal life?

Is that low season trip to Thailand during monsoon season worth the risk?

Is the depreciation of the car I like versus the slower depreciation of a car that I'm not so crazy about worth the possible loss in trade-in value?

Is moving to another apartment in a neighborhood that I may like more worth the risk of maybe ending up with shitty neighbors when I like the ones I have now?

Is the man sitting in front of me on a date worth the risk based on what he's telling me? For example, he recently broke up with his boyfriend. Or worse, he still lives with the "ex" boyfriend.

On dates, when I get around to them that is, I find myself unable to stop running the guys against some mental check list to figure out if they…you guessed it…are worth the risk.

Does he seem hung up on an ex?

How long has he been out compared to me, and does he still have wild oats that need attention?

Does he live within ten miles to me? Because let's face it, I hate driving long distances on a regular basis.

Will his lack of always chewing with his mouth closed drive me so nuts I may want to scream at the top of my lungs one day in the middle of a meal at Antoine's?

Is he cuter than me? And if so, can I risk my somewhat jealous tendencies?

So many questions running through my mind. *All the time.* No wonder I can't sleep. No wonder I'm on Prozac for anxiety. Each day is one long careful thought about is *it*, *this*, *that*, *him* worth the risk.

It's a Tuesday evening. I'm being wild, for me, by being out on a work night. It's actually a nice June night in New Orleans. The humidity isn't too oppressive. The stars twinkle above. I have a nice glass of Merlot I'm sipping while sitting across from a reasonably cute guy.

I've actually managed to snag a date. Okay, a friend set me up, but still. We met up at a cute outdoor wine bar in the Bywater I've been meaning to check out. Sounds good, no?

The guy's name is Bailey, and he's a paralegal. Check the box off next to the line item that reads "Sustainable Career." He has wavy dark hair and blue eyes. A lethal combination to make my heart skip a beat. Check off the box next to the line item "Feel at least an inkling of sexual attraction."

He actually asks some questions about me. *Woohoo!* Check off line item "Seems interested in getting to know me as a person."

I tell him about growing up in the Garden District and my time spent backpacking across Europe and trying to find myself right after college. And then...

"You know my ex went backpacking across Europe," Bailey says, his gaze suddenly appearing to be focusing on some point far, far in the distance. "He said it was the best time of his life."

Uh, oh. Please don't make me check off a line item in the column for "Run as fast as possible."

"Have you ever been to Europe?" I ask, trying to bring the conversation back to...you know...*us!*

"No. But, Tim, my ex, said that he loved Sweden most of all. He always had a thing for blondes. Maybe that's why..." Bailey says, his voice trailing off.

Please. No.

I'm not even half-way through my glass of wine, and this guy is making a mad dash for my personal "move on" line-up.

"Hmmm. I've never been to Sweden. But I've always had a thing for guys with dark hair," I say not so subtly dropping what I would think would be a huge ass hint.

"We lived in New York for a while. Before we broke up, and I moved back here," Bailey says, swirling the Merlot in his glass around and around.

"I still haven't been to New York," I say. "I was thinking maybe of taking a trip there next fall. Any recommendations?"

Come on, Bailey. You can do it! You can move back into the "maybe" column. For the love of God! *Come on!*

"Everything is amazing there. *Everything,*" he says still looking off into the distance. "I remember when I was flying back here after we broke up. I thought to myself how can you leave this city and this *man* that you love so much?"

Shit. I know it's happened now. We've moved into the so not worth the risk because he's hung up on his ex-boyfriend to the point that he doesn't even realize he's told you more about his ex than himself.

I lean back in the wicker chair I'm sitting in, sip my Merlot, and look up at the twinkling lights in the sky. I start to tune out Bailey as he starts in on how he met the ex.

Oh, well. Maybe the next guy. *Maybe.*

Chapter Two- Troy

"Two more damn days, man. *Two!* You hear me? Then we're out of this boring, hot ass desert," Eric said to me as we both watched some of our fellow soldiers carry supplies to a nearby tank.

"Can't come fast enough," I said, putting some sunblock on my face. It felt like I stayed sunburned here no matter how much of the crap I spread on my skin.

All of us were feeling the sweet anticipation of this tour finally coming to an end. Two years felt like twenty.

"What's the first thing you gonna do?" Eric asked me.

I knew the first thing I'd *like* to do, but I still had no idea if it was even a possibility. After all, neither one of us had talked about what happened that night when the two of us were on a patrol. Eric and I had found ourselves alone, behind one of the tents at the camp, and we reached out to each other in a way I thought could only be a fantasy where he was concerned. I still didn't know exactly if it was just a *moment* for him or if he felt the same way I did.

We'd had each other's back through this whole tour. He was a Southern boy just like me. He came from a small town in Alabama, and we found we could relate to each other in a lot of different ways. I don't know if I would have been able to make it if it hadn't been for his easy going personality and ability to keep my laughing in the shittiest of situations.

When I met him upon arriving in Afghanistan, I had just started coming to terms with who I was…who I had been running from all these years. But the moment I saw him, there had been no more doubt. With his red hair, light freckles, blue eyes and compact muscular body I immediately felt my heart flutter, and I knew I was in trouble. I had one of those moments I had thought were just bullshit when other people talked about them…love at first sight.

"So?" Eric said, waiting for an answer.

I turned and looked him in the eye. No one else was close by. Do I dare say something? I looked down at my boots trying to gain courage to say what my heart longed for. When I looked up, he was gone.

"Eric?" I called out, looking around.

He'd suddenly disappeared on me.

"Eric? Where'd you go, man?"

Then the explosion. Loud. All consuming. A bright flash of light.

I scream out, *"Eric!"*

I sat straight up in bed. The clock read eleven at night. Sweat poured off my forehead and my heart raced. Slowly, everything started coming into focus around me. My brother Louie's new seventy-two inch flat screen, family pictures on the wall, the mismatched furniture.

"Christ," I muttered under my breath. I had fallen asleep on the couch watching some bad sci-fi movie on cable.

The dream again. There almost was never a night that it didn't haunt me.

I rubbed my eyes and got out of bed for some water. I'd learned not to try and go right back to sleep as it often led to me just picking up the dream where it left off.

While heading for the kitchen I peeked into my brother's bedroom and saw he still hadn't gotten in for the night. Almost thirty, Louie was still a party animal. He'd tried to get me to go out with him, but I didn't feel like hanging out in a bar on Bourbon watching people flirt, laugh, and drink. It amazed me each and every time that other people had no apparent awareness of the crap happening on the other side of the world at that very moment. Since coming back this time, I couldn't shake those thoughts, but it was that sense of how precious life was that finally made me be honest with myself.

I turned on the faucet and poured myself a glass of water. I could hear the sounds of jazz music drifting in the air from a club down the street from my brother's apartment on Burgundy. I headed to the second floor balcony off the living room and stepped outside to get some fresh air. Being back home in New Orleans still felt strange. So much had happened before I returned home that it some-times felt like I saw everything through a different set of eyeglasses than everyone else.

The sound of laughter mixed with the jazz, and I wished I could return to that kind of state of simplicity. I wasn't even sure I could stay in New Orleans long-term. My instincts told me to keep running farther and farther. Maybe if I did long enough the pain of the past and the awkwardness of the present could be left behind.

I sat down on a semi-rusted lawn chair Louie had found on the street and dragged upstairs. Louie. With all his eccentricities, he was an amazing brother, and I was lucky to have him. When I came out to him he didn't miss a beat. I just knew that he'd be shocked over his Army brother, former high school football quarterback, and ladies man coming out of the closet.

Instead all he did was take a drag on his joint and say, "That's cool, man."

"That's all? You…got nothing…else…you know…to say?" I stuttered, completely surprised at his non-reaction.

He had shrugged his shoulders and said, "Nah. I just want you to be happy. That's all. When are you going to tell mom and dad?"

"Dunno," I had answered.

The truth was I wasn't sure if I *was* going to tell them. My dad was a retired NOPD detective, and my mom was president of the Catholic Women's League of New Orleans. I didn't know if they could handle having a gay son, and I was conscious to the fact that I had been distancing myself from them as a result, too.

"They're gonna shit, but they'll get over it," Louie said, cracking a smile.

I wished I had been as confident as him about my parent's ability to accept the fact that their son wasn't…had never been…exactly who they thought him to be.

In retrospect, I should have known that Louie would be accepting. He ran in artist circles in New Orleans and his best friend since first grade was Elliot a guy who had been out of the closet since high school.

Scared to go back to sleep and risk being taken back to a world I fought to left behind, I decided to go back inside and channel surf a bit. A part of me began to wonder if I should have gone out partying with Louie and his friends. Maybe a few drinks would have calmed my mind and helped me forget.

Just before I sat on the couch, there was a knock on the door. I had no clue who it could be at this hour unless Louie came back early and had forgotten his keys.

Chapter Three- Elliot

"Oh, hi," I said, thrown off when a muscular hand-some god opened Louie's door. It took a few moments before it registered who stood before me. He was as handsome as ever, but now there was an added maturity to him. "Troy?"

"Elliot! Long time, no see. Come in," he said, opening the door wider for me to walk inside.

"I'm sorry...I...uh...wanted to bring back Louie's camera. He's such a night owl. I thought....Well, I hope I didn't wake you up or anything. I didn't know you were in town."

I found myself feeling hot and flushed all of a sudden. I had always had a crush on Troy growing up. He had been Louie's older, dreamy brother. Over six feet tall, coal black hair, emerald green eyes, and a wide killer smile that would leave you breathless. *My first big crush.* Sure, Louie and I had been close friends since elementary school, but when I hit puberty, around the time Troy must have been a senior in high school, I came up with an endless supply of excuses to visit Louie's house in the hope of just catching a glance of his brother.

Everybody in school knew of Troy. He had been the big man on campus from first grade to graduation…quarterback, dating the head cheerleader, most likely to succeed at…well…*everything*. I used to practically swoon if I happened to walk by him in the halls at our tiny Catholic school, and he'd say, "Hey, Elliot. What's up?" to me. This walking sex on a stick would actually acknowledge me…little freshman me. It made me feel special each and every time.

He'd joined the military right after high school. Louie said his brother wanted to give back to his country in this time of war and crisis which of course made him even more swoon worthy to me. When he came home he usually stayed at his and Louie's parents in Mandeville about an hour from New Orleans, and I hadn't seen him in years now.

"No problem. Come in," he repeated.

I tried to pull myself back together. *Damn.* In a matter of seconds, he had turned me back into a shy awkward teenager.

"Thanks," I said, finally walking inside. "Is he here? I just stopped by on the off chance to return this."

I laid the camera on the coffee table, and then nervously stuffed my hands into my pockets.

"Nah, he went out with some friends. He hasn't come back in yet. You want anything to drink?" he asked.

"Ah, that's okay. I should probably be heading home myself. I borrowed his camera for a trip I took to Puerto Vallarta. I never get around to buying a good digital camera myself. Why should I when I can borrow Louie's, right? I just left meeting up with a da…friend, and since he's always up late, I thought I'd stop by to see if…"

Dear God! I'm rambling. Someone stop me please before I embarrass myself even more!

"You know, see if he was home."

Finally. I shut myself up.

"I'll make sure he knows you dropped it back by," Troy said. He started to open his mouth again as if he were about to say something else. Then, he paused for a bit before saying, "So, how you been all these years? When I've asked about you, Louie says you've been working as an…uh… actuary here in town."

He's asked about me! Don't. *Stop.* Please don't further embarrass yourself by reading more into a casual conversation.

"Yeah, for a few years now. I've never made it too far away from New Orleans. Sort of stayed close to home. How are you? Louie said you were finishing up with the military. He didn't say you'd be in town though."

"Yeah, I sort of surprised him. I was going to travel around for a bit before you know…making my mind up about my next move. But I decided I should spend some time with my little brother."

"That's great. Maybe I'll see some more of you while you're in town. Any idea on how long you'll be here?"

He shrugged his shoulders, and I couldn't help but notice how his blue t-shirt pulled tightly in all the right places.

"I'm still figuring some things out. What the next move is. Stuff like that," he replied.

"Cool," I said, momentarily unable to think from the impact of gazing at him. "Well, I better head home and let you wind down. Thank Louie for me again."

"Sure. I..." Troy started to say before trailing off.

I stood there waiting for him to finish. Why did Troy look so nervous? I could never recall seeing him look nervous about anything. Then again, it had been a long time, and I couldn't even imagine some of the things he must have gone through in the middle of a war zone."

"See you around," he finally said.

I had the nagging feeling that that had not been the phrase on the tip of his tongue.

"You, too, Troy. Take care," I said, walking out and shutting the door behind me.

Damn. Some guys just got better looking with age. As I walked back down to the street, I wondered what he had been about to tell me...and what had stopped him.

Chapter Four- Elliot

The next day, I headed to my friends', a couple named Mason and Joey, for brunch and a little volunteer work. Joey was head of a local HIV prevention organization called NOLA Aware, and coming up soon was their biggest annual fundraiser, the Summer Sizzle Fling and Flung. I'd been helping out with the event the past few years and had grown to look forward to it. The work gave me a sense of satisfaction that my corporate number crunching never gave me.

"Wow! Elliot, you've outdone yourself," Joey said, reviewing the list of silent auction contributors I had managed to put together including a very generous donation from Saks and numerous antique shops on Royal Street.

We sipped our mimosas while sitting on their balcony and waiting for Mason to bring out the food.

"Thanks. I just want to see us even top what we did last year," I said.

"You're really good at fundraising," Joey said. "You should do it full-time, you know?"

"After having to take and pass all of those actuary tests?" I said, laughing off the suggestion.

"Something to think about," Joey said, winking.

"So, we want to hear all about your date with Bailey?" Mason said as he walked out and set down a platter of cheese and crackers.

"He's a cutie, isn't he?" Joey, says as he sips his Shiraz. Joey looks pleased with himself and confident that his matchmaking plot succeeded.

"He was cute...and interesting," I say before taking a sip of my own wine. I so didn't want to disappoint them. Joey knew Bailey from the law firm he used for the non-profit. He'd been trying to set us up for weeks until I finally gave in.

"Uh, oh! *Interesting*. That doesn't sound *interesting* in a good way," Mason said. He passed out cloth napkins to us, and I noticed how he poured Joey more wine without him having to ask. The gesture made me think it really was the little things that mattered the most. What I wouldn't give for someone who'd go ahead and pour me a little wine without being asked, give me a back rub after a tense day, or bring home a freaking three piece from Popeyes knowing I wouldn't want to think about dinner that night. Was it all too much to ask?

"Oh, no! You didn't like him!" Joey said frowning. "I just knew you two would be a great pair."

Mason set next to Joey across from me, and I thought to myself how they just seemed to *fit* with each other. Physically, they were quite the opposite. Mason had a pale complexion, slim frame. Joey's bi-racial background gave him envious light mocha skin, and he had an athletic build. But their personalities just appeared to complement each other. One always seemed to know what the other wanted or needed. I didn't know if I'd ever fell that kind of intimacy…or even open myself up to the possibility.

"Don't get me wrong. He was nice, but…" I said.

"But? Come on. Tell us," Mason said, ready for the scoop.

"He seemed a little preoccupied with his ex-boyfriend."

"Ummm," they both uttered in unison.

"He talked more about his ex than himself. I'm not sure I could tell you three things about him after spending two hours together," I said, before letting out a big dramatic sigh. "Thanks though. I appreciate it. Maybe it's just not a good…"

"Oh, maybe Morgan from my office," Mason said, perking up. "He's handsome in a Tobey Maquire way, and he just bought the cutest little Fiat."

"One of those little cars that you expect a dozen clowns to climb out of?" Joey asked.

"They can park in any spot," Mason replied. "I'll put feelers out on Monday."

"No, no! That's okay. I think I need a little break," I said. The last thing I wanted was another set-up.

"But…" Mason started to protest.

"Really. I'm okay," I said firmly but as nicely as I could.

Mason looked disappointed and said, "You'll let me know if you change your mind, right?"

"Definitely," I said, putting on my best smile. "I just think I need a date break."

"I just can't believe you haven't met or seen any guy who piques your interest," Mason said, before popping a cheddar topped cracker in his mouth.

My mind went back to Troy from the night before. Damn. *He was hot.* But...

"Oh, wait!" Joey said, sitting up straight in his chair. "He's seen someone who got his motor running!"

"Nah," I protested.

"He has!" Mason said, agreeing with his boyfriend. "Tell us! Who is it?"

"It's impossible," I protested.

"Nothing is impossible," Mason said. "Not when it comes to *love.*"

"He's straight!" I said. "Straight as a board. No chance. *Nada. Nein.*"

"Oh, good Lord. Don't tell me you're lusting after a straight guy," Mason said, shaking his head.

"For God's sake!" I exclaimed. "I'm not lusting after anybody. I just...uh...last night..."

Damn it. I couldn't even believe I was even talking about this it was so utterly crazy.

"Last night what?" Joey said.

"I dropped by my friend Louie's apartment last night," I began.

"Oh, my God! You have a crush on Louie! Haven't you two been friends since childhood?" Joey asked.

"Well, we first met when we were young," Mason said to Joey.

I groaned loudly and said, "I do not have a crush on Louie, okay?"

"Well, then who are you talking about?" Mason asked looking confused.

"Louie's older brother, Troy, was at his place last night. He's in town after finishing a stint in the Marines."

"*Marines?* That sounds hot," Joey said.

"I always had a crush on him growing. But he's straight. *Straight.*" I emphasized.

"A Marine. That's sexy," Joey said, before turning to Mason and saying "Remember when you had me wear that uniform..."

Mason must have kicked Joey under the table because he said "Ouch!" all of a sudden.

"The point is that...well...there is no point. He's handsome and polite and positively swoon worthy, but he's straight. So, no point in even going there."

Joey and Mason gave each other a look that suggested that the two of them weren't totally convinced.

"So, what about floral arrangements?" I said, trying to change the topic. "I have a connection with a florist out in Old Metarie."

"You're really good at all of this event planning stuff," Mason said, echoing what Joey said earlier. "You ever think about doing it full-time?"

"Told you," Joey said with a satisfied grin.

Chapter Five- Troy

By the time my brother stumbled out of the bedroom from his post-party night drinking/hangover, I had already spent three hours scouring the online job ads looking for something decent to apply for. After years of having the military telling me where to go and what to do, the idea if having so many possible options was sort of overwhelming. The truth was after going through many years feeling confident in my decisions and paths I was stumped for the first time. I didn't know what the hell I wanted to do.

"There's still coffee left," I said to Louie, who looked like the walking dead.

"Um," he groaned. He walked into the kitchen, grabbed a mug, and poured a piping hot cup of wakefulness.

"Your friend, Elliot, dropped off your camera last night."

Louie just nodded.

"Had fun last night?" I said, closing my laptop. I couldn't look at one more job posting that day. Maybe I would take a run along the river. The humidity was enough to make you feel like you were walking through soup, but I needed to burn off some energy as that often helped me focus.

"My head feels like it's going to crack open in half," Louie said. He plopped down on the sofa across from the small dining table where I sat. "Had a blast..."

"You're not as young as you used to be, little brother. It's going to catch up with you," I said, realizing I sounded like our parents. When did that start happening?

"Yeah, thanks for the reminder," Louie said, slurping his coffee. "What are you up to?"

"Trying to find a job. There's not much around though. Maybe I should head to Houston or Dallas."

"You just got here! You can't leave yet!" Louie pleaded, and for a moment, he reminded me of the little boy he had once been who always wanted to tag along with me wherever I went.

"Need work though," I said matter-of-factly.

"Give it time. It'll happen," Louie replied. "Besides don't you need to stick around for a while and have *the* talk?"

"What do you mean?"

"Oh, I don't know," he said, setting his now empty mug on the coffee table. "Dad. Mom. You being into guys. *The talk.*"

"I told you. I'm not sure I'm even ready to tell them."

"You have to sooner or later," Louie said, shaking a finger at me.

"Why?" I protested. "Maybe they don't need to know."

"You're their son! Of course, they need to know. Maybe they already have a clue anyway."

"Yeah, dude. No. I don't think so," I responded. I couldn't imagine my dad the retired cop and my cookie baking mom even entertaining the thought that their Marine son was gay. Not. Going. To. Happen.

"You never know," Louie said, shrugging. "And don't you want to just get it out in the open and off your chest at this point? Are you scared?"

Scared. Hearing the word sounded like nails on a chalkboard to me. I didn't like to think of myself as scared of anything...not after everything I'd already seen during my tour of duty.

"I'm not scared," I insisted. "I'm just not sure they need to know right now."

"Um, hmmm," Louie muttered, irritating the hell out of me. "I think you're scared, and I just don't understand how..."

"How what?" I demanded.

"How you can have gone off to a war zone and seen and dealt with things I can't even imagine, and yet you're scared to tell your mom and dad you like boys."

Feeling my face reddening, I stood up and said, "You don't know shit, Louie. You're right about one thing. You can't imagine the crap...the human destruction...I've seen over the past few years, and the last thing I need is my little brother the perpetual party animal judging me."

I immediately felt a little sorry for my choice of words, but I didn't feel like apologizing at that moment, either. I grabbed my wallet and keys and said, "I got to get out of her for a bit."

"Troy!" Louie called after me, but I didn't turn around.

I stormed out of the apartment and headed down stairs to the street royally pissed off. But a little part of me deep inside did feel a little embarrassed that I still felt any shame about who I was...and I was scared to tell my parents. How could I shatter everything they thought they knew about me?

Chapter Six- Elliot

Grocery shopping, or as we say in New Orleans "making groceries" is not an easy task. If you don't feel like driving out to the burbs where all the big box stores were located, you were stuck shopping at places like Carnival Zone, a store whose layout was as perplexing as a David Lynch film. Tomatoes next to the tampons? Okay. Maybe we're going for something alphabetical. Then there was the *supermarket*, to use the term loosely, on Royal in the Quarter that used to be an A & P. It had to be the world's tiniest grocery with aisles seemingly built for hobbits they were so narrow. And the selection and the prices left a lot to be desired, but again...not many choices. Sometimes I just didn't feel like driving the car and leaving the neighborhood. One of the things I loved about living in the Quarter the most was that I could accomplish most of what I needed and wanted to do by walking.

The Quarter supermarket was where I was at trying to decide between the three kinds of available cereal when my phone rang. I pulled it out of my pocket and saw it was Louie probably wanting to thank me for returning his camera.

"Hello?" I answered, pondering whether I should get the high fiber cereal I need or the sugary marshmellowly brand I wanted.

"Thanks for dropping the camera back off, dude," Louie said.

I could tell from his voice alone it had been a long night. I knew him that well.

"Thanks for letting me borrow it. I posted the pictures online. Check them out."

"Cool," he said, pausing a moment. I also could tell he wanted to ask something of me by his tone.

"What's up?" I asked, deciding on the sugar rush cereal. Screw healthy.

"I know you saw Troy last night."

"Yeah, that was a surprise," I replied. A really *hot* surprise, I thought. But I would never tell Louie I lusted after his straight brother. "Your parents must be happy to have him back."

A tiny, older lady, maybe in her eighties gave me a dirty look to move out of the aisle so she could get in, so I quickly moved around the corner.

"Yeah. Both Mom and Dad are over the moon, but I'm not sure how long he's staying."

"Ah, okay."

I knew Louie was still dancing around what he wanted to ask, and I didn't have a clue as to why.

"I was wondering if it would be okay if I gave him your number. I thought maybe the two of you might...hang out. He might could use some advice from you right now."

Advice from me? I couldn't imagine about what.

"Uh, sure. Of course. What's up?" I asked.

"Just...he's trying to decide some next steps with parts of his life, and I think you might be able to help."

I wondered if he was thinking of taking an actuarial exam to start a new career.

"Excuse me, but you're in the way!" the little lady said in a shrieking voice.

"I'm at the Royal Street market blocking traffic..." I started to say.

"No need to say anymore," Louie replied.

"But, of course, give Troy my number. He can call anytime."

"Thanks, man," Louie said before hanging up.

I headed to the checkout where the cashier wore a thin party store looking blonde wig haphazardly on top of her head...you have to love New Orleans... and I felt myself getting just a little bit *too excited* at just the thought of talking to Troy on the phone. I needed to rope this one in ASAP because it could only lead me down one road...disappointment and heartbreak.

Before I made it to the check-out line, I remembered to pick up a box of my cousin Pat's favorite cookies. Pat, my mom's first cousin and quite the eccentric, lived in the Bywater, and he usually checked on my apartment when I went out of town. He was getting up there in years, and I was his closest family since my parents retired in Mandeville, a suburb of New Orleans. So, I tried to check on him frequently, too.

The cashier with the blonde party wig avoided eye contact as she scanned my items. *Sassy* customer service in the Quarter was the norm. I paid and checked out without her saying a word to me and headed out of the market.

Once on the street, I heard someone call out my name. "Elliot!"

I turned around to see an old co-worker, Leslie, making her way down Royal Street towards me. I used to *love* working with Leslie. We'd sneak out for long lunches sometimes, dish the latest gossip, and discuss our current men trouble which there always seemed to be a plentiful supply of any day of the week. She ended up moving on to a company in Houston a few months ago.

"Girl!" I exclaimed.

"Hey, babe!" she said, throwing her arms around me and pulling me in for a bear hug despite the bag of groceries between us.

I always thought Leslie missed her calling as a runway model. African-America, six feet tall, legs for days, piercing dark eyes, and gorgeous natural curly hair that framed her heart shaped face.

"What are you doing here?" I asked. "Couldn't stay away from the Big Easy, huh?"

"You know I gotta visit my mama and 'dem on a regular basis if I know what's good for me," she said. "And I've been missing you! I've got no one to share a fried oyster salad with at lunch."

"Those oysters were the best," I said.

I really had missed her *so much*. Our work was sometimes less than exciting, and it was amazing the difference one person could make in livening up an atmosphere for you.

"Well, then you should come to Houston. We've got a few openings coming up. I was going to call you while I was here to see if I could talk you into a move."

"Really?" I said, my interest piqued. I'd tossed the idea back and forth for a move, but it never felt like just the right time. Leslie had never been one afraid to take risks though. A new job in Houston might offer a step up the corporate ladder. She wouldn't hesitate. She always grabbed life by the balls.

"I'm tight with the HR manager, too. I know I can get you in. What do you say?"

I wish I could just jump at new opportunities like she did.

I ended up having a drink with Leslie at a nearby bar. Only in New Orleans would someone sit on a barstool with their bag of groceries sitting on the seat next to them. It was great catching up, and I promised her I would think about the offer. Maybe a change of scenery was needed right now. Sometimes I felt like my life was in a rut...doing fine...but not really going anywhere.

On the way home, I stopped by my cousin Pat's in the Bywater to give him his cookies. He happened to be outside working on his mini-flower garden on his side of a shotgun house, a home built decades back where one room leads to another to another to another, with an open door throughout. The name coming from the fact that you could shoot a gun and have the bullet go straight through the house. His miniature pet pig, Poncho, that he loved walking along the river, rooted his nose in a nearby patch of ground.

"Hey there!" I called out.

"Well, there you are!" he exclaimed, standing up. He wore a large yellow sunhat and overalls. Head to toe he was barely five foot three. Seventy-one years old now, he loved telling me about the old days in the gay bars of the Quarter and the men he knew and loved. "Poncho and I were just talking about you a few minutes ago and wondering how you were."

I looked at Poncho rooting around in the dirt and tried to picture him carrying on a conversation with Pat. I couldn't help but let out a little giggle.

"I didn't know Poncho was such a conversationalist," I replied.

"Oh, yes. You wouldn't believe the deep discussions we get into," Pat said in a serious tone.

I just nodded. Better not to question. I held out the box of double chocolate covered vanilla wafers Pat loved.

"For looking after my place while I was in Puerto Vallarta," I said.

"Well, ain't you a sweetie," he said, taking the box of cookies. "Come in for a spell and have a cup of tea with me."

I had a million errands to run, but somehow I could never turn Pat's invitation for a little company down. After a drink with Leslie and now this, my produce would be completely wilted by the time I got home.

"You came at just the right time. I was going to start painting the kitchen floor later," he said, pulling off his gardening gloves.

Painting the kitchen floor? Again, better to not ask.

He took Poncho to the backyard and threw a pile of cut up vegetables at him before leading me into the kitchen.

"How was your trip? Tell me about the boys," he said, a twinkle in his eye.

"There were some cuties," I said, sitting down at the kitchen table. "I just wasn't feeling it much though."

"Hmmmm," he muttered, putting a kettle on to boil. "At your age I was *always* feeling it. We need to get you fired up again. Maybe set you up on a nice..."

"Oh, no! Not right now," I replied.

God, why did it feel like everyone was trying to match me up?

"You better use it before you lose it," Pat said, always the wise one in his own way.

"I ran into an old co-worker who thinks she could get me a job with her company in Houston if I wanted it."

"Houston!" Pat exclaimed. His voice went up three octaves. "Think of the cowboys!"

"I don't know. It'd be a big move, and I just feel..."

"Feel what?" Pat asked. He set out a small plate of some of the cookies I had brought with me.

"Something needs to change. I had hoped the time I spent in Puerto Vallarta would have cleared my head and gave me some new perspective."

"And?"

"And...not much has changed."

"Maybe you do need to shake things up a little bit."

"Maybe," I replied.

But would it be worth the risk?

Chapter Seven- Troy

When I opened my package of forwarded mail sent to Louie's house, I felt like I had been kicked in the stomach. There it was. A small little envelope made of fancy grade paper addressed to "Mr. Troy Chandler and Guest." I had a sinking feeling I knew what it was, and I dropped it on the table like it was a hot potato. I had heard rumors from mutual friends and online social media, but now I knew this would make it real.

Finally, I decided to act like I had some balls and open it up. *Confirmed.* There was an invitation to Eric's wedding to his high school sweetheart Danielle. Ever since the day of the explosion of the road side bomb where I thought I may have lost him forever, I had been promising myself that I would tell him how I felt and be damned the consequences. At least I would have been man enough to tell him.

But as he lay in the infirmary recovering from scrap metal hitting his legs from the explosion and I sat next to him telling him everything would work out and he'd make it home, I could never summon up the courage.

"If something does happen to me, and I don't make it back..." he began to tell me the day after the explosion.

"Don't say that!" I said. "You're making it back. We're *all* making it back."

"But if..."

"Eric," I groaned.

"*If*...okay? I need to say this. After what happened yesterday, you just don't freaking know. I need you to do something for me."

Just the thought of something happening to him, of both of us not making it back, was enough to tear me up inside. But I knew from the look on his face that he needed me to hear this.

"We're both going to make it back home. *Safe*. But go ahead if you need to," I finally said.

"If I don't make it back..." he said, pausing and taking a deep breath. "I need you to make sure and tell Danielle that I always planned to marry her when I got back home, and I want her to move on without me if she has to. It's what she deserves."

At that moment, it felt like someone had kicked me in my stomach, and I sucked in a breath. I couldn't deny it to myself. As much as what happened that night meant to me, it didn't mean the same to Eric. If it did, he was nowhere willing to admit it. My deepest hope of maybe the two of us finding our way together once we left that desert shithole went right out the window.

"Sure. Of course," I had said hoping that I put on my best game face. I knew then I couldn't allow myself to fantasize anymore. The night where the two of us had touched each other and made each other feel better...at least for a moment...had been just that...*a moment.*

I felt as alone as usual.

And now, Eric had invited me to his wedding in Memphis. The thought made me feel queasy, but I tried to shake it off. I should be happy for him. He'd made it back, and he would get to marry Danielle.

I slumped down on Louie's couch and wondered what to do with the rest of my day. Louie was rehearsing with his band, and I was putting off seeing my parents for another day.

That invitation brought up all of those feelings I had had before of feeling alone...isolated.

I noticed a sticky note stuck on my wallet on the counter. I knew it was some sort of message from Louie. My brother was obsessed with sticky notes, and he would leave them in the oddest places sometimes.

I got up walked over and read the message.

"Call Elliot and say hi. He's been there," the noted said with a phone number scrawled underneath.

I sighed. Maybe I should give him a call. It certainly couldn't hurt trying to make some gay friends here and maybe get me out of Louie's apartment some. There was something that felt odd about reaching out to Elliot though. I'd known him his whole life. He'd spent many weekends at our house growing up spending time with Louie. Yet, I didn't really know him all the same.

I decided finally to stop being a wuss. I picked up the phone and started to dial.

Chapter Eight- Elliot

"I'm gay."

I really thought I was beyond someone really being able to shock me. I thought I had already seen and heard it all before. After all, I live in New Orleans. But Troy almost made me choke on my bottle of Jax when he uttered that one short little sentence.

When I got his phone call asking if I'd be up for meeting and grabbing a beer I admit I felt a little twinge of excitement. Troy and a beer all to myself. It was practically a wet dream! But then I brought myself back down to Earth and remembered that it would be just two "dudes" hanging out and drinking brewskies. Maybe he did want to pick my brain about possible career options. But then he suggested we meet at a bar on the 800 block of Bourbon. I paused and wondered did he know that the 800 block of Bourbon is where the gay bars started. How could he not though? He grew up in New Orleans. Then I decided maybe he was just offering to meet up somewhere he thought I'd feel extra comfortable, but...hmmm....odd.

When I walked towards the bar we agreed to meet up at I saw him standing outside, looking slightly fidgety, wearing a gray tank top and board shorts. His muscled tattoos were all on display. He looked even tastier than he had the night before. I couldn't help but feel that this meeting, that phone call, the location all seemed odd and unexpected.

"Hey. Hope I didn't keep you waiting long," I said, when I walked up to him.

A look of relief swept over his face when he saw me.

"Hey, man. Thanks for meeting me," he said, hands in his pockets.

"No problem," I replied.

We stood there in silence for a couple of seconds as a group of drunk tourists stumbled past.

"Want to go inside and grab that beer?" I suggested.

He looked like he could sure use one. What the hell was up?

"Yeah. Let's do that," he said.

He went in first, and instead of heading to the bar downstairs, he made his way to the back stairs to go up to the second floor.

Just like he knew where he was going.

No. Couldn't be. But hello???

When we got upstairs he ordered a couple of beers and tried to make what sounded like some very forced small talk about the weather, how the Saints might do in the fall, and how my family was doing.

We then headed out to the balcony which was empty this early in the evening and sat down on a bench. He took a long swig of his beer, and that's when he said it.

Chapter Nine- Troy

I just blurted it out to him. I didn't know how else to go about it. I felt sort of silly that a grown ass man such as myself still had problems uttering those words to someone, but the truth was it still scared me. When you fight so hard against your nature for so long to embrace it doesn't just happen overnight even if we'd like to do so. There's too much history of making up stories to placate others, watching what you say, where you look to just wipe that all away in one swoop. I had worked so hard at trying to appear not to be gay for so long it had burned itself into my subconscious.

I looked at Elliot for a reaction. I still half-expected people to fall out from shock or something.

"Really?" he said. "Wow."

"Yep. Gay. Gay. *Gay*," I said, letting out a bit of a forced chuckle.

He didn't say a word for a moment, but instead, just set their quietly taking it all in I guess.

I felt so nervous I could vomit right then and there. I don't know why, but I just did. I don't know what I expected him to say. I mean he's gay himself.

"I didn't know," he finally said. He stared at me for a moment and blinked. He looked like he was choosing his next words carefully.

"Does Louie know?" he asked.

"Yeah. I told him about six months ago. In a freaking email while I was in Afghanistan if you can believe that. He suggested that I talk to you. You know since..." I trailed off.

He smiled and said. "Since I'm gay, too, of course."

I noticed what a nice smile he had. A smile that sort of put you at ease.

"Yeah," I replied, starting to feel a little more relaxed. "I don't really have any gay friends here. Everyone here knew me before I joined the military."

"I'm not usually shocked by anything," Elliot admitted. "I guess since I grew up around you I figured I would have picked up on something like that. I mean...I thought I had great gaydar. Maybe it's not as sharp as I thought."

We laughed.

"Maybe not," I said.

"Do your parents know?" he asked.

"Hell no!" I said, a little too strongly. "I mean...I haven't told them yet. I'm not sure when I will...if I will."

I started feeling uncomfortable again with the topic of my parents. The thought of disappointing them overwhelmed me. I knew they had such a clearly defined vision of who and what their soldier son was. I'm not sure they could ever reconcile the fact that I'm gay with their thoughts of me and their conservative values. Hell, Louie's "hippieish" life was enough to leave them perplexed and sometimes exasperated.

Elliot nodded quietly. I think he sensed I had more to say but was struggling to get it out.

"I mean I've seen a lot of crazy shit the past few years in the war. Stuff no one should ever have to see. The stuff people will do to each other…over what…it blows your mind. So, you learn not to really think about it. To push the feelings deep inside you because if you tried to face them then and there, you'd never make it through your day. You learn…*not* to be emotional."

I stopped talking, took a sip of my beer, and stared down onto the street.

Elliot took a breath and said, "Sounds like everything you've been through might create a mindset that would make it even more difficult to come out and sort through your feelings."

"Yeah, it's true," I replied, relieved he appeared to understand.

"Well, I think you're very brave," he said, locking eyes with me. "*I mean it.*"

"I don't feel so brave," I admitted.

"Don't be so hard on yourself. Coming out is never an easy process for anyone."

"How can telling my parents be scarier than any of the crap I've been through the past few years?"

"Maybe..." he started to say, before pausing a second. "Just like you said. During the war, you sort of taught yourself not to feel about what was happening around you. With your parents that's probably going to be impossible."

"You're right," I admitted.

"I know everything you're going through is hard, Troy. But it will get better," he said, placing a hand on my arm.

"Promise?" I said, trying to smile.

"Yeah, I promise," he said. "I'm glad you called me, too."

"I didn't want to bother you or anything."

"You're *not* bothering me. Whenever you need to talk give me a shout."

"Thanks. That means a lot right now," I replied, and for once, things did feel like they may actually be okay eventually after all.

Chapter Ten- Elliot

Holy crap. *Troy's gay!*

I kept replaying the conversation I had with him as I walked back to my apartment on Burgundy. We agreed to meet up at least by the following weekend. I'd introduce him to some more people stuff like that.

But damn.

To find out that the guy who had been my boyhood crush was gay, and I had no idea. Well, my mind started to spin. God, I wanted to hold him and kiss him so badly when we were sitting on that balcony together and tell him everything would be okay.

Stop. It.

First of all, the guy was barely peeking out of the closet. Plus, guys that look like him always go for...well, guys that look like him. There was no way anything could happen beyond some friendship and me helping him in the coming out process. That's the way it would be. And, after all, who can't use another friend. Right? But damn. How I wished it could be more.

I took out my phone and texted Louie.

WTF? I had no idea.

About a minute later, a message from Louie popped up.

I know. Thanx for talking 2 him. I worry bout him right now.
I sent a message back.
Sure. Anytime.

At work the next day, I spent most of the day just star-ing at my computer screen, not getting much done, and thinking about Troy's confession.

"Elliot?" I heard my boss, Suzanne, say behind me. She snapped me right out of my fantasy where Troy admits his secret, everlasting love for me.

"Oh...hi," I stammer, swiveling around in my chair.

I swear the woman must have magical feet. I never heard her walking up to my cubicle, and of course, she always managed to stop by when I looked less than pro-ductive.

She sighed loudly in her passive aggressive way to let me know that she wasn't too impressed with what she had just walked up upon. Suzanne, in her smartly tailored conservative pant suits, was all business, all the time.

"How's that report coming along for the Hughes Foundation?" she asked. "Our meeting is this afternoon, remember?"

"Of course," I lied.

Oh, shit. I forgot.

"I'm almost done with it," I said, lying for the second time.

She nodded, not looking entirely convinced.

"Good. I'll see you in the conference room at three then," she said, before silently walking away.

I quickly pulled up the report I should have finished by now and started running numbers. My phone rang, and I cursed under my breath. The last thing I needed was someone wanting something else when I was already running behind.

"This is Elliot," I answered.

"Hey, boy!" Leslie said on the other end.

I let out a breath of relief.

"Thank God it's you," I whispered into the phone. "Silent Suzanne just caught me spaced out when I should be finishing up a report."

"You're burned out on that place," she said.

"Yeah, I know," I said.

"Have you given any thought to my offer to put in a word for you? My boss was just saying this morning that they're getting ready to open the position."

"I'm thinking about it. *Seriously.*"

"Well, you need to do more than think when the position opens. The amount of resumes they got for the last one was mind-blowing," she said.

I heard another phone line ringing in her background.

"I've gotta go. Call me later," Leslie said, before I heard a click.

I tried to turn my attention back to Silent Suzanne's report, but my mind kept drifting back to Troy.

My cellphone buzzed, and I pulled it out to find a text message from my mom. Ever since she learned how to text, she's been going crazy with it. When I touched the screen to open the message, a feeling of dread came over me.

The message read, *"Let me know how the date goes."*

Date?

And then I remembered, somehow I had allowed myself to be set up on yet another date for coffee. This time it was by my mom through a friend of hers. I know I should feel lucky that my mother is so open and accepting of my being gay to the point that she's become a relentless matchmaker. I groaned...a little too loudly for the office. But then I thought to myself that maybe this was just what I needed to take my mind off of this longtime Troy crush.

As my mother once said, "The best way to get over a man is under another one!"

Chapter Eleven- Troy

"Turtle soup," my mother said, shaking her head. "Why would anyone do that to a poor turtle?"

My dad just grunted in response as his eyes scanned the menu for something that was familiar.

I didn't know what the hell I was thinking taking my parents out to dinner to someplace where the menu would like Greek to them. To come out to them would be enough of a jolt to their systems. Bringing them to the new Cajun-Asian fusion restaurant in the Quarter was not going to help things. Maybe I thought they'd be distracted by the food to the point of not fully registering that their military son sleeps with men.

"I don't know what the hell any of this is, son," my dad said, putting the menu down. "Can't I just get a po-boy?"

He wore his usual faded black t-shirt and baggy jeans. His silver hair was cut in a high and tight. I swear he looked the same practically every day as far back as I could remember.

My mother, on the other hand, was in one of her glittery blouses, light blonde hair teased up within an inch of her life, and she nervously tapped her fingers on the table. She quit smoking just two weeks ago, and I know she's wound up so tight on a nicotine withdrawal she'd throw Mother Theresa under a bus for a drag on a Marlboro.

Seriously, I don't know what the hell I was thinking with this set up.

My stomach felt like someone was grabbing it and then twisting it in the palm of their hand over and over.

Finally, after all three of us ordered the least perplexing thing on the menu, some Cajun version of fried rice, I decided I had to do it right then and there or I would lose my nerve.

"Mom. Dad," I started to say.

"Did you see the prices on that menu?" Mom said cutting me off. "Highway robbery and for food I don't even understand."

"Yep," my dad said, nodding his head in agreement. "Nothing like you can cook up at home."

"Easy for you to say," Mom said back. "The key is you don't have to cook it. I'll eat whatever if it means I don't have to turn on that stove for a night."

She then turned to me and smiled sweetly.

"It's sweet of you to bring us out for dinner, Troy. You didn't have to," she said, reaching over and patting my hand. "You know us. We're just not used to anything but what we've always known."

I know, I thought to myself. That's why this would be so hard.

"How's the job hunt?" Dad said, all business. "You know I could still put in some calls..."

"Thanks, Dad. But I'm still not sure I won't to stay here in the long-term."

"But why not?" Mom asked. She tapped her fingers in a more hurried pace. "You've got your whole family here. We've barely seen you the past few years with your tours of duty."

Dad reached over, and in a rare moment of affection slapped me on the back and said, "We're proud of you, son. Serving our country. Made us real proud. Now if you could just kick your brother's ass in gear."

"Louie's doing fine," I said. "He just follows the beat of a different drummer."

"Yeah, a tone deaf drummer," Dad replied, shaking his head.

I feel myself losing my nerve. With each second that goes by, it slips further and further away from me like I'm in the ocean and each wave carries me further and further out from land...from courage. Anything outside their usual and my parents freak. There's no way they're going to take this well.

"Be nice," Mom scolded Dad. "Louie is just finding himself."

"Well, I wish he'd hurry up and do it. He's not getting younger," Dad said before turning to me. "Speaking of which, when are you going to find yourself a nice sweet girl and settle down."

That's it. I feel the waves of fear take me out too far away to get back to my goal. I can't do it. I've seen innocent civilians killed in roadside bombs. I shot an enemy combatant at point blank range with no hesitation. But now I feel five years old again, and I'm scared what I'll say will make my parents not love me anymore.

"I don't know, Dad," I respond. "One day I guess."

I'm pissed at myself as I walk back to Louie's apartment.

Chicken shit.

I spent the rest of the dinner with my parents making bullshit small talk about possible work leads, what the Saints might do in the fall, the weather, hell, anything besides what I really meant to share with them. They headed home after dinner but not before expressing shock over the total bill even though I treated. Now I'm just disappointed in myself. I can feel the anger at myself rising up in my throat like a poison.

I picked up the pace walking on the sidewalk ignoring the pleas of a man sitting on a plastic crate who swore he could tell me where I got "dem shoes."

An old Chevy backfired as I turn onto the 300 block of Bourbon Street. The sound made me involuntarily jump.

A memory flashes through my mind. Unbearable heat from the sun beating down on me. A gun fired at me. A few inches to the left, and I'd probably be dead.

I tried to shake the thoughts off. I can't remember. Not now. Not here.

A group of loud college kids stumbled by me and headed into a straight karaoke bar. Deep down I know for some reason it's not a good idea, but I head inside to get a drink anyway.

The bar is packed wall-to-wall with people who at least look like they're having a good time. Bartenders moved non-stop trying to keep up the volume of drink orders that comes with people one hundred percent focused on getting shit-faced. A college-aged girl wearing the world's shortest pink skirt and halter top screeched into the microphone about how she couldn't get any satisfaction.

I noticed a group of young military guys with their tell-tale high and tight haircuts in the corner. They hooted and hollered at the girl with the pink skirt while a group of other young women wearing too much make-up vied for their attention with tight shirts revealing ample cleavage.

I wondered how many nights I had been in bars just like this one getting drunk with guys in my unit. I always tried my best to appear like I was interested in the girls…just like the other guys. Ass grabs. Drunk kisses. Whatever it took to do what I thought would finally make me feel like I fit in, but I never did *fit*. Now, I didn't feel like I belonged in this world or the so-called "gay world" but was stuck in some sort of awkward middle. I was just as uncomfortable living my life as I was before.

I made my way to the bar through the crowd to order a drink at the bar. Whiskey. Neat. I slugged it back and ordered another one…and another.

The girl with the pink skirt is replaced on the stage with a trio of bottle blondes singing a Britney Spears song. Some of the military guys, hormones surging, made their way to the stage and held up dollar bills in their hands as if the girls were strippers.

The alcohol hit my system faster than expected, and I began to feel as if the room were slightly spinning. *Shit.* I realized that I didn't really eat much of anything with my parents, and I had skipped breakfast since I had been too nervous about meeting with my parents to eat. Waves of nausea overtake my system, and I looked around for the nearest bathroom.

About ten minutes later, my head pounded and my jaw ached from the hard punch I received from one of the military guys. I stumbled down the street trying to get away from the bar as fast as I could. Everything happened so fast. One moment I'm trying to get to a toilet before I puked, and the next some guy is screaming at me for supposedly touching *his girl.* How ironic is that? I never saw the first punch come my way, and before I could hit back, a bouncer grabbed me by the back of my shirt and jerked me towards the front of the bar and pushed me out the door.

I didn't want to head back to Louie's. I couldn't take the questions I knew he'd have if he was home. I had told him earlier my intentions to come out to our parents. Now, the night had gone from bad to worse. I tried to keep my balance as I made my way down the sidewalk among the tourists and partiers that now crowded the streets. Their shouting and laughing made my head throb even worse. I touched my now sore cheek. The swelling would come on soon enough.

I didn't know where to go next. And then I thought of Elliot.

Chapter Twelve- Elliot

Have you ever been on a date with a phone? Because it's happened to me quite a bit lately. If you're wondering what I mean, let me describe my latest unsuccessful attempt at a romantic date.

My mom's friend from a women's exclusive gym set me up with her nephew who lives in town. Yep, it's gotten to *that* point.

Reluctantly, but figuring I didn't have much to lose at this point, I agreed to meet up with the guy at a cute little cafe on Frenchman in the Marigny for a cafe au lait. At first look, I was pleased. He was reasonably cute with sandy blonde hair, dark chocolate brown eyes, and a trim torso.

We ordered our drinks and sat by the window, a perfect spot to watch the eccentric world of the Marginy walk by.

"Thanks for meeting up," the guy, John, said.

"Sure," I replied.

"You're cute. You never know who's going to show up in these situations."

I felt myself blush. I had a hard time accepting compliments.

"Thanks. You're cute, too."

"I heard you're an insurance salesman," he said.

"Actually, I'm an actuary," I replied. "We work with..."

And then my real date appeared....*the phone.*

A buzzing sound had John frantically digging into his jean pocket to pull out a cellphone.

"Sorry," he said. "I just need to check..."

He started typing out a text message wildly before placing the phone on the table.

"So, yeah. Insurance. How did you get into that?" he asked, his gaze focused on his phone with the intensity that one might stare at a ticking time bomb that was set to go off in three seconds.

"Actuary. Not insurance," I corrected him for the second time.

"Cool, cool," he said, briefly making eye contact. "I'm into home design. I never know when a new client might call, ya know?"

"How long have you been doing that?" I asked.

His eyes, obviously waiting for his cellphone to pop back into life, fixated on the two by five screen.

"Uh, a few years now. I went to school for..."

The phone vibrated, and he scooped it up like a pot of free gold sitting on the table.

"I'm sorry. I've got to take this one real quick," he said, picking up the call and, as a result, raising his voice about three levels. "This is John....Hey...I'm great...Nothing much..."

As he rattled on with whomever was on the other end of the phone, I realized I could probably leave at that very moment, and it would probably take him a good ten minutes to realize I'd disappeared.

I sipped my cafe au lait as I recalled that I did have that marathon of *Revenge* episodes on my DVR to watch. Just as I was about to slurp down my drink and excuse myself, he hung up the phone, looked at me, and said, "So where were we? Sorry about that. A friend of mine back in Ft. Lauderdale. It's so hard to find the time to connect with people these days, you know?"

I shrugged and sarcastically replied, "You think so?"

Sarcasm lost.

"No, *really*," he said earnestly, placing his phone back on the table. His gaze focused on it with an even higher level of concentration. "Sometimes it feels hard to just have time for a decent conversation."

"I think I might now what you mean," I replied dryly.

"I could never sell insurance," he said. "I don't think I could live on commission. How do you do it?"

I took a deep breath. *Really?* I thought about telling him for the third time that I didn't sell insurance. But, then I decided to see just how much he *wasn't* paying attention. "It's tough. It's not easy trying to convince people to buy insurance for their shoe collections."

He nodded non-committedly and said, "Yeah? Cool. Cool."

And then his phone buzzed again.

After enduring fifteen more minutes of watching my date talk on his phone with brief periods of asking me again about my non-existent insurance career, I motioned that I was headed to the bathroom. But with a new level of being *over it* I instead bypassed the bathroom and walked out of the cafe to head home. I wondered how long it would take him to notice I'm gone. At least twenty minutes. Maybe more. If my mother hears I left the guy behind, I'll tell her I had food poisoning and had to bolt for the bathroom. No one asks anymore questions when you tell them that excuse.

It was getting past eight o'clock, and the summer time air felt as thick and warm as an electric blanket resulting in me lazily walking down the residential streets of the Quarter. I decide to head down Dauphine and maybe pick up some take out at that new Cajun-Asian fusion place that sounds so intriguing. But when I got close to the restaurant, I saw through the window Troy and his parents.

His mother was talking wildly, his father looked bored, and Troy looked like his new puppy just got run over by an eighteen wheeler. I sensed that it wasn't a good scene, and since they haven't seen me yet, I turned around and headed in the opposite direction. I wondered if this was the night Troy was going to work up the nerve to tell his parents.

Poor guy. As much as mine drive me nuts, they embraced the *gay me* pretty quickly even joining the local PFLAG.

Troy's parents had trouble wrapping their mind around Louie's life so I can imagine how they might be finding out he's gay.

I decide to call him later that night to check in.

As a friend.

That's all.

Really.

"Holy shit," I say when I open my front door and see Troy standing there looking disheveled. His button down shirt is half tucked in half hanging out. His jaw line looked bright red.

"Hey," Troy says, slightly slurring his words. "I'm sorry. I just...I couldn't go home right now. And I remembered Louie pointing out your place when we walked by the other night."

"No problem. Come on in," I say moving aside. "Are you sure you're okay?"

He walks in and sways a small bit. I grab onto his arm and lead him to my leather sofa where he sort of collapses.

"It's been kind of a rough night," he says.

"I can tell," I say sitting next to him. I look closer at his cheek and say, "Were you in a fight?"

"Just a little one," he replies as if it's not a big deal. "Some asshole in a bar on Bourbon. Thought I was hitting on his girlfriend. Ain't that ironic? I was just trying to get to the bathroom. Thought I might vomit, and I almost tripped and fell on the girl."

"Jesus," I muttered. He looked so vulnerable, lost. I wanted to put my arms around him, pull him close, and tell him it will all be okay. But I shouldn't. No matter how much my instincts tell me to do so. "Let me get some ice for your face."

I patted him lightly on the arm before getting up and heading into the kitchen. I remembered I had no ice, so I pulled out a frozen bag of green beans I purchased probably a couple of years back. When I got back to the living room he'd taken off his button down and stretched out on the couch. His right arm is above his head stretching his white t-shirt revealing not only his impressive biceps but a tattoo of rose and a cross on his upper arm.

"Here," I said, kneeling down next to him and placing the bag of frozen beans on his cheek. "This will help keep the swelling down."

I felt sorry for him. This big strong guy who I always thought of as looking confident and assured looked so lost.

"You're sweet," he half-whispered before adding, "Tonight was so fucked up."

"What happened?" I asked, before quickly adding, "You don't have to talk about it if you don't want to though."

He looked at me eye to eye, and I felt butterflies in my stomach just from being caught in his gaze.

"I tried to tell them, but I couldn't," he said softly. "I wussed out."

"Don't say that," I reply. "You didn't wuss out. It's not an easy thing....coming out."

"Still..." he mutters, and I sense his strong disappointment in himself.

"I know it might be hard to believe right now, but things will get better."

"Not with my parents," he said, shaking his head.

Before I even realize I'm doing it, I placed my hand on his chest and gently stroked his pecs. A quick look of surprise swept over his face.

"I'm...uh...sorry. I didn't mean to..." I stammered.

Unexpectedly, he grabbed my hand as I tried to pull it away.

"It's okay," he said, his eyes meeting mine. "You're sweet."

I knew he was still drunk, and as much as I wanted to lean in and kiss him, I couldn't do that with the shape he was in currently.

"Just being a friend," I said. "Anytime you need to talk."

Troy squeezed my hand, and it felt like his touch sent a bolt of electricity through me. My defenses were weakening as he continued to gaze into my eyes.

Can't do this now. You don't want him to regret something afterwards.

"Why don't you just crash here for the night?" I offer.

For a brief second, his eyes widened.

"I'll get you a blanket and a pillow for the couch," I quickly added. "You might as well just sleep things off here."

For a moment, he looked deflated. Then suddenly he leaned in and placed a kiss on my lips…first gently and then with more aggressive passion. I gave in to him and began to start kissing him back, our tongues intertwined. It's a boyhood crush finally coming true.

But just as quickly as he pulled me in for one hell of smooch, he pulled away and sat up.

"Oh, my God. I'm so sorry," he muttered.

He stumbled and stood up leaving me feeling and probably looking a little stunned as I was still knelt down by the couch.

"Uh, it's okay," I said, standing up.

I should have stopped it when it started. He didn't mean it. It was only the alcohol.

"I really should head back to Louie's," Troy said, avoiding eye contact. He ran a hand through his hair and tried to smooth down his shirt. "Thanks for letting me come over and for…you know…listening."

"Sure. Any time," I said, taking a deep breath and trying to regain my composure. As fast as my real life fantasy started it ended.

"Thanks, Elliot," Troy said.

He turned around looked at me one last time. I thought he might say something else, but instead he just reached for the doorknob and walked out.

I slumped down into the couch.

This sucked.

Chapter Thirteen- Troy

The next morning I woke up to a pounding headache that felt like someone was hitting a cast iron skillet up against my head over and over. My tongue was dry and heavy in my mouth, and an annoying stream of sunlight shined through a crack in the curtain.

Hangover from hell.

I willed myself to sit up on the sofa bed in Louie's apartment. The clock on the wall read a little after noon.

"Well, hey there, sleepyhead!" Louie's booming voice ratcheted up my headache a few notches. "I was wondering when you'd wake up. Hard night?"

He's dressed in a vintage Che Guevara t-shirt and ripped jeans which was almost a formal look for him. He must have been heading out somewhere.

"Wanna come join me and some friends from the band for some crawfish?" he asked.

Just the thought of peeling crawfish was enough to make me hurl right then and there.

"God, shit, no. But thanks," I grumbled.

"Are you sure?" he asked, eying me suspiciously.

"Yeah, I think I need to just take a shower and chill out."

"But it's the Fourth of July. You can't just stay home all day. Where's your fucking patriotism?"

Fourth of July. I forgot.

"It's got a bad hangover," I answered.

He cocked an eyebrow and said, "Did you and Elliot go out looking for dudes last night?"

Ah, hell. I did not want to talk to my little brother about my love life…or lack thereof. It still seemed weird.

"No. I didn't go out looking for *dudes* with Elliot," I said, shaking my head.

Then in a flash it came back to me. The kiss. Oh, shit. I went over to Elliot's drunk and then practically forced a kiss on him. *Shit.* What he must think of me now. I made a total ass of myself.

"Well, you can't stay home all day and night. It just ain't right. You're coming out tonight with me and some friends to see the fireworks at the river."

"But…" I started to protest.

"Sorry! Can't hear you!" Louie said, heading out the door. "I'll be back to walk over at about eight tonight."

He then slammed the door behind with the sound making my head feel like it's going to crack open.

"Crap," I muttered. I stood up and headed into the bathroom for a cold shower.

I had just started to become friends with Elliot, and it was nice having someone that got where I was coming from. As supportive as my brother was he still couldn't completely "get it."   But now I probably screwed that friendship up.

Good going, Troy.

Chapter Fourteen- Elliot

"Come on it'll be fun!" Joey insisted. "A few drinks, fireworks."

"I don't know if I'm feeling it this year," I said.

I was having a shrimp and grits brunch with him and Mason at the Quarter's drag queen cabaret slash restaurant named Belinda's at Savannah's.

"It'll be fun," Mason said. "You can't stay home on the Fourth of July!"

As much as I loved them, having brunch with my favorite couple wasn't making me feel better today. Instead, it just filled me with more disappointment at Troy practically tripping over himself to get out of my apartment after he gave me a drunken kiss...a kiss I stupidly allowed myself for a second to believe it could mean a lot more. The two of them just reminded me of the elusive romantic relationship I could never seem to develop with anyone.

"I'll think about," I finally answered, very non-committedly.

"What you thinkin' about?" a booming voice said from behind.

I turned around to find Miss Althea, drag queen extraordinaire and co-owner of the restaurant and cabaret. She wore a yellow sundress with white roses on it. Her hair was teased higher than gravity could possibly ever allow, and she wore huge gold hoop earrings. Rumor had it she was in her seventies now, but you would never know it. And you sure as hell would never *ask* her how old she was. Her light cocoa brown skin still appeared almost completely free of even a hint of wrinkles. Miss Althea's performances on the stage at the cabaret had made her a French Quarter legend, and I swear she knew everyone who lived within a five mile radius. She had been a good friend of Mason's Aunt Savannah who passed away years before, and as a result, she acted as his and Joey's honorary "aunt."

"We're trying to convince Elliot to join us for the fireworks tonight, but he's being a party pooper," Mason said.

"You're too damn young to be sittin' it out already," Miss Althea said, playfully slapping me on my shoulder. "Hell, even me and my *huzzzband* will be there. And you know I'm just a tad past forty myself. Why don't you bring that hunk of a man I saw you out with the other night?"

"Hunk of a man?" Joey and Mason said in unison.

"Who are you talking about, Miss Althea?" I said.

"That fine military lookin' perfected piece of a man you's out with at the bars the other night," she said.

Troy. Did anything happen in the Quarter that she didn't know about?

"Who is this?" Joey asked. "You're holding out on us."

"We're just friends," I insist. "It's Louie's brother I told you about."

"Well, I tell ya one thing...just friends wouldn't be what was up in my mind if I had that muscle god next to me. You need to lay claim before somebody else beat you to it, honey."

"We're just friends," I repeat.

All I thought about since he practically sprinted out of my apartment the night before was that kiss that sent me to heaven...and then to heartbreak hell...in a matter of moments. I wondered if he'd tell Louie. Ugh. Nah, probably not. Even though he initiated the kiss, it somehow felt like my fault. I should have pushed him away. He was drunk, and he didn't really know what he was doing. Plus, it felt kind of nice with the two of us becoming friends, but that was probably shot to hell after that moment of awkwardness.

"*Just friends,*" Miss Althea repeated. "If I had a dollar for every person that said that but ended up in bed with their *friend* I could retire."

"You'll never retire. You'd hate it," I said, playfully and trying to change the subject for God's sake. I didn't need any help thinking about what happened the night before.

"Well, I'd never want to disappoint my fans. That's the truth! I'll probably be up on that stage lipsyncin' some Diana Ross holdin' on to a walker for dear life, baby! But I see you boys wastin' the handsome years all the time, too scared and shy to make a go of it with someone they want. If you want that military man, you need to go for it…and *go big*! Now, I better get back to preparin' for rehearsals for the new show. I got a couple of new queens. Damn, they a handful!" she started to head to the backstage area, but turned around and looked back at me sternly. "You listen to what I say now!"

I smiled, and she walked behind the heavy black curtain on the stage in the back of the restaurant.

"You should listen to her," Mason said, nodding his head.

"So, what time for the fireworks?" I said, trying again to change the topic.

Maybe it would do me some good after all to get out tonight versus just sitting home and thinking about that kiss…and how badly I wished it would happen again.

Chapter Fifteen- Troy

"Your brother's hot," one of Louie's female friends, Margo, said. She had more tattoos on her than I've ever seen on a woman. Tattoos covered her arms, legs, neck, and even a shamrock under her right eye. Her curly obviously dyed black hair framed her pale face giving her an almost ghost-like appearance.

"Well, he doesn't play for your team. So, don't get any ideas," Louie said, his arm wrapped around his girlfriend of the month, a Goth chick named Gigi.

I shoot Louie a dirty look. Ever since I came out, it's like the first thing he says to anybody about me as if that's all there is to say. I know I should feel glad that he feels so comfortable with me being gay. Maybe he's more at ease with it than me, and that sort of bothers me.

The sun has just gone down, and we're sitting on a bench on the Moonwalk along the Mississippi River waiting for the fireworks.

"What a shame," Margo says, running her fingers along my bicep. "But I've always thought the idea of two guys getting it on was *hot*."

"Uh, thanks," I mumbled, not sure what else to say.

His indie musician friend, Guy, with the spiky bleached hair and nose rings said, "Hey, what the hell about me?"

"What about you?" Margo snorted. "I've always had a soft spot for Marines."

She smiled seductively, obviously unable to take a hint.

"Pimp juice?" Margo said offering everyone some of the frozen daiquiri she bought in a gallon container.

I've been gone just long enough to find it strange that there's no open container law here.

"Yeah, I'll have some," as I reached for a red cup full of the fruity alcoholic beverage. I needed something to steady my nerves. Civilian life still felt foreign to me in a way. As crazy and unpredictable life in the Marines was it had become my norm.

The crowds along the river grew quickly until everyone was elbow to elbow. The muddy smell of the river drifted through the air, and the humid air almost felt like a hot, wet blanket...very different from the dry desert air that had been home for so long.

When Louie said we'd be meeting lots of his friends I asked if Elliot would be there, but Louie told me he thought he had plans already. I found myself wondering if he had a date, and then I remembered it was none of my business. I still couldn't believe that I had kissed him like that, but I had to admit that the memory of the kiss still lingered in my mind. Elliot had green eyes that sparkled when he smiled and a self-acceptance about him that I envied and found attractive.

Boom.

The first fireworks exploded in the air releasing bright red and blue lights in the night sky.

People around me began to clap and whoop and holler in enthusiasm.

"More?" Louie said, nudging me and holding up the container of daiquiris.

I shook my head no.

Boom.

Green, yellow, and purple.

Extra loud boom.

Beads of sweat began to gather on my forehead, and I tried to wipe them away in vain.

Boom.

My stomach began to twist into knots,

Flashes of light. Screaming.

"You all right?" Louie said, squeezing my arm.

I turn to look at him, and I see a look of concern on his face.

I start to nod yes, but then...

Boom.

In the desert. Scorching sun. So hot I can't catch my breath.

Louie shook my arm and said, "Hey, bro! Okay?"

My heart beats so fast I think it may explode right out of my chest.

Boom!

"Get down! Get down!" I scream to one of the guys, no more than eighteen years old, who looks stunned into not moving.

I reach out to grab him and pull him down to the desert floor when a flash of light knocks us down to our knees.

"Troy?" Louie said, shaking my arm harder.

I noticed his friends looking at me know. They all have the same look of concern and confusion on their faces.

Boom. Flash. Screams.

Sweat now poured off my forehead and under my arms.

I look at Louie and said, "I'm sorry. I've got to go,"

I turn around to try and force my way out of the crowd.

Louie grabbed for me and said, "Wait!"

"I'll be okay," I call back as I started to make headway. "Promise. See you later."

Louie looked scared, so I tried to give him a little smile to let him know I'd be okay.

It took a good fifteen minutes, but I finally broke out on a small stretch of sidewalk on Decatur that wasn't packed. I tried to catch my breath, but my breathing was still labored. I saw a break in traffic and I run across the street to the opposite...off to somewhere, anywhere else.

Chapter Sixteen- Elliot

Just as Mason, Joey, and I crossed Decatur towards the river, I saw Troy about a block down bolting across the street like he was on fire. Once he made it across, he leaned against the wall outside of a restaurant.

Mason and Joey catch me staring across the street at him.

"Who's that?" Mason asked, cocking an eyebrow.

"Louie's brother," I replied.

"Wow! He is handsome," Joey said, followed by a playful elbowing by Mason. "Just an observation!"

"He doesn't look so good right now," I said.

Even from a distance I could tell he appeared lost and confused. How could that be though? He was raised in this city.

"I'll catch up with you guys. I'm going to check on him."

"Should we come with? See if he's okay?" Mason said, concerned.

"That's okay. I'll try and catch up with you guys," I answered.

"Sure?" Joey asked.

I nodded and said, "Yeah. Positive."

Mason and Joey continued towards the river as I made my way across the street. It took a few seconds of me standing right next to him before he noticed my presence.

"Hey there," I said.

Troy was pale and beads of sweat had formed on his forehead.

"Uh, hey," he said, quickly straightening his posture when he saw me. I half expected him to salute me.

"Are you okay? You look a little...off," I said.

"Yeah, I'm cool," he said, but his voice cracked, betraying him.

"I was just heading towards the fireworks with a few friends. You want to join us?"

"Thanks, but I just came from that way. I think I'm going to head back to Louie's to chill out for the rest of the evening."

I got the strong impression that there was much more to the story here.

"What happened? You really don't look well," I said. "I saw you bolt across the street."

He took a deep breath and said, "Yeah, I guess the noise of the fireworks just doesn't agree with me."

There was a loud explosion and a flash of light from the fireworks at the river, and I saw Troy tense just for a second.

"You want to go grab a drink or something to eat?" I asked not wanting to leave him alone.

"Uh, I'm okay. You go catch up with your friends," he said, wiping the sweat off his forehead.

"It's not like I haven't seen the fireworks before. I'll text them and tell them I'll meet up with them later. Come on. Let's go grab a bite. What do you say?" I asked, smiling. Instinctively, I reach out and squeeze his arm.

Troy relaxed a bit and said, "Are you sure? I don't want to keep you from anything."

"Positive," I answered. "Come on. Let's go grab some good old fashioned greasy food."

He smiled and nodded.

A few minutes later we were sitting at a tiny table in the Clover Grill on Bourbon Street watching our burgers being cooked under one of their famous hubcaps.

"You want to talk about it?" I asked before adding quickly, "If you don't, it's okay. I understand."

He took a long gulp of his Coke and swirled the plastic straw around in his drink.

"I'm sorry. It's none of my business," I said.

"No, it's okay," he replied. "Sometimes...certain noises, sounds, and lights sort of take me back to some of my time in Afghanistan."

"Oh..." I mumbled quietly. "I'm sorry."

"It is what it is, you know?" he said, picking his paper napkin into tiny pieces. "There was a guy who...meant a lot to me. I thought he died in one of the roadside bomb explosions."

"Was he okay?"

"He had some injuries, but he made it through. Scared the shit out of me though."

"I'm sure. I can't even imagine," I said, pausing before adding, "When you say the guy meant a lot to you were you..."

"In love?" he said unexpectedly.

"Yeah."

He nodded before adding, "I was. Crazy in love and for a time I thought he might feel the same way. But he got engaged not long after that close call...to a woman."

"Oh," I said. "I'm sorry to hear that."

"Wasn't meant to be, you know? Sometimes the hardest thing in life is to just simply accept things for the way there are. But I still have nightmares sometimes about the stuff I saw and experienced."

"Here ya go, handsomes," the young waiter with fire engine red hair and a twinkish body said while setting our burgers and fries in front of us. "Need anything else?"

"I think we're good," Troy said.

"Oh, baby, I can tell you're *good*, but did you need anything else?" he said, obviously captivated by Troy's rugged attractiveness.

Troy chuckled and said, "I'm okay. Thanks."

"Well, you let me know," the waiter said, winking before heading over to some customers sitting at the counter.

"Somebody has a crush," I said teasingly.

"I don't know about that," Troy said, pouring ketchup on his fries.

"I do. But you must know how handsome you are," I said, surprised at my boldness.

Troy blushed and looked down at his plate. "I don't know what you're talking about."

"Okay. Sure. Whatever," I said, nudging him playfully.

I couldn't believe this new flirty, bold me especially after swearing to myself that trying to pursue anything with Troy was a bad idea times a hundred.

"You want to go fishing tomorrow?" Troy asked suddenly.

"Fishing?" I repeated, taken off guard.

"Yeah, an old buddy of mine is lending me his boat for a couple of weeks. I thought I might take it out to Lake Ponchatrain tomorrow. If you're off, you know..." he said, trailing off.

I did take the next day off for a long four day weekend. I had thought I'd spend the day parked in front of the TV watching bad made-for-television movies on Lifetime while gorging on ice cream. Every now and then I just needed a day to do *nothing*. But fishing? The last time I was on a boat, my uncle's party barge, I got seasick just from the small waves we encountered. Me, water, and boats had never been a good combination, but when I looked at Troy, who appeared vulnerable all of a sudden, I knew what I would do.

"Sure. That sounds great!" I said, lying right through my veneered teeth.

"Great!" Troy said. His expression perked up considerably. "I was thinking of taking it out kind of early though before it gets too hot. Like maybe six tomorrow morning."

Six a.m. Dear God!

I had never been a morning person, but I managed to force a smile and said, "Sure. That sounds fine. Sounds like fun."

"Great," Troy replied, picking up his burger.

I wondered what I was allowing myself to get into as I felt all of my usual reservations being overridden by something else in my brain...feelings I was both excited and scared to death of having.

The next morning, Troy picked me up at 5:30, and before I knew it, we were out in the middle of the lake.

"Isn't this great?" Troy called back to me as our boat plowed through some rough waves.

I gave a thumbs up and tried to smile. I double-checked under my seat to make sure the life vest was there...just in case. I inhaled the salty, humid air in an attempt to calm my stomach while the wind whipped through my hair making me realize that making sure each hair was just so this morning had been a completely pointless activity. With each two to four foot wave the twenty foot boat hit I thought I might upchuck my morning coffee.

Willpower. Willpower!

I guess God decided to have some mercy on me as Troy finally began to slow the boat down.

"I think this might be a good spot," he said to me as the boat thankfully slowed to a stop. He cut off the motor and threw the anchor out.

I glanced at my watch and saw that it hadn't even hit seven o'clock yet. What oh what had I gotten myself into?

"Are you okay?" Troy asked. "You're looking a little pale."

"Just need some more coffee," I replied, trying to smile even though my stomach was still in knots. I pour another cup from the thermos of caffeine Troy had thankfully thought to bring along with the bottled water and sodas.

"Thanks again for coming out with me this morning," he said with a smile that could melt even the hardest of hearts.

"Sure. Thanks for inviting me."

My stomach finally began to settle as the boat settled into a soft rocking motion.

"I haven't had the chance to do this...in years. There was a many a day out in the desert that I wished I was out here on the lake again."

I knew I would never have a complete idea of what he went to while on duty. I'd never lived beyond two hours of where I lived now. Even with the dangers he faced, a little part of me was envious that he had gotten to see more of the world while I had just stayed here.

He took out the fishing rods and opened a small bag and pulled out some live squiggly worms.

Oh, God. Not my stomach again.

"Want me to bait your hook for you?" Troy asked, the worm helplessly wiggling between his fingers.

"Yes, please," I replied.

I didn't think I had it in me to pierce it with the hook.

"I can't remember the last time I did this," I said. "I must have been a little kid. My grandfather used to take me to the seawall where we'd fish. He died before I turned ten though."

"You haven't said much about how your family is now," he said, handing me the rod now properly baited.

"My parents moved into a condo over in Mandeville a few years back. My sister, Miranda..."

"I remember her. She was a couple of grades ahead of me."

"She moved to Los Angeles after college. Works in movie development now. Although, I have to admit that I still don't really know what that means, but she seems happy. My cousin Pat is my only family left in the city. I check up on him every now and then. He's always quite the...hoot."

After he finished baiting his hook, Troy asked, "You remember how to cast it?"

I looked down at the reel and realized I didn't remember at all. So much for appearing sporty and outdoorsy.

"Hmmm...I might need a refresher," I admitted.

"It's like this," he said, standing behind me close, just a mere couple of inches between us. It felt like my heart rate increased ten-fold.

He placed his hand on mine on top of the reel. The touch felt like an electric shock to my system.

"Hold down this button," he said, pressing his finger down on top of mine. "Take the rod back behind you. Bring it back around and quickly release."

My line with the doomed worm went flying out in the water.

"See. Nothing to it," he said, walking back over to his own rod and reel.

I could've landed Jaws at that moment. All I could think about was how it felt to have him so close to me again.

We sat there for a couple of hours, slowly reeling our lines in and making general conversation. I told him some about my work and how I thought about making a move sometime soon since I didn't feel challenged anymore. He told me about his thoughts of going back to school and earning a degree but he wasn't sure what he would want to get it in.

The summer heat and humidity began to creep up on us. I knew I was getting nasty sweaty in my t-shirt and cargo shorts. I could sweat even when an AC was on high, so I could only imagine how wilted my appearance had become since we left that morning.

"The heat is on now," Troy said, lazily reeling in his hook.

"I know," I said, wiping the beads of sweat off my forehead.

Then, he quickly lifted his Saints t-shirt over his head revealing a toned, muscled chest with light dark hair.

Oh, shit.

I tried to keep from reacting too much and staring but the desire was too strong. He had a naturally worked out chest that came from rigorous physical labor versus the gym which made me feel even more inadequate. I had always been thin but not exactly toned.

Before I had a chance to stare too much the line on my reel grew taut and the line began to spin out of the reel.

"Oh, crap! I've got something!" I said, trying to hold onto the rod. I was afraid the fish on the other line would jerk the rod right out of my hand. "I think I'm going to lose it!"

Troy quickly got behind me and placed his hands on top of mine again.

"Keep reeling it in. Nice and steady," he said.

Every few inches of progress got lost as the fish would then pull back on the line.

"Jesus! Do I have Shamu or something?"

"You can do it. You just have to wear it out," Troy said.

I could smell his scent, a mixture of soap and sweat, and I felt the heat from his body pressed up against mine only the thin fabric of my white t-shirt between us. It was practically intoxicating to the point where I forgot about the fish on the line.

"Keep reeling," he said, his voice steady.

I could care less about reeling in my big catch, but if it kept him next to me I was more than happy to reel this in all day long.

Finally, there was a break in the water, and out popped a tiny six inch or so speckled trout.

"What the hell?" I exclaimed. "That's it?"

Troy burst out laughing.

"There's your Jaws," he said. "Let me get the release hook so we can let it go. It's too small to even think about keeping."

He released his blissful grip on me and headed to the back of the boat.

"Try and keep it in the water," he instructed.

"I can't believe that's what was about to pull me out of the boat," I said, shaking my head and slightly embarrassed.

"You'd be surprised by their strength," Troy replied, returning with the de-hooker. He dipped his hand in the water and carefully backed the hook out of the fish's mouth.

I was struck by how gentle he had been in releasing the fish. In one quick movement, the fish took off back into the water to fight again one day.

"You did that like a pro," I commented. "I'm impressed more by you than the size of my fish."

"Didn't they ever tell you size isn't everything?" he said, winking.

I felt the back of my neck heat up, and I knew I was blushing.

Damn. I could give myself away so easily.

"Here. I'll bait your hook again," Troy said, taking my rod and reel from me and sitting in the chair next to me.

"Thanks," I replied.

He took a deep breath and started to say something but then stopped.

"What is it?" I asked.

He looked up at me and said, "I'm going to tell them. I'm not going to chicken out again."

"Your parents?"

He nodded.

"You know you can wait if you need more time to feel comfortable."

He shook his head and said, "I can't put it off any longer, or I'll just keep putting it off. I want to get it over and done with."

"Well, if you need to talk afterwards, you can give me a call…or stop by," I said.

"I appreciate that," he said. He was silent for a moment before adding, "And the way you handled my drunken kiss the other night. Well, thanks for not holding it against me."

I laughed a little nervously at the mention of the kiss. "Don't worry about it. I actually, well…"

"Well what?" he said, cocking an eyebrow.

I decided to summon up all my courage before I had enough time to change my mind about it. I took a breath and said, "I didn't mind it really."

"*Really?*" he said. His face broke out into a huge smile. "That's nice to know."

"You know…it was…cool," I said, trying to sound all nonchalant now.

"Just cool?" he asked, his eyes gazing into mine.

I started to tell him it was way more than cool, but then that nagging voice popped up in my head…the one that reminded me he was a newbie and probably way out of my league in the end. I tried to tell the voice to shut up, but it drowned out any other thoughts I had in my head.

"Yeah, it was cool," I said noncommittally.

He gave me a smirk, but didn't push the subject.

"Here ya go. All nice and baited again," he said. He handed me the rod and reel. "Go ahead and cast it out. You never know what you might catch."

He winked at me. *Winked.*

I swallowed hard and turned my gaze back to the water and cast my line. He was just being a little flirty to be nice. *Don't read more into it. Just don't.*

We stayed out on the water for another hour or so staying mostly silent and falling in to a nice steady rhythm of casting and reeling in. Neither one of us caught another fish, but it was okay. I couldn't remember the last time I felt so comfortable just being with someone.

We started to pack up, and Troy pulled up the anchor. He told me that he had a lead from a buddy on some house remodeling job he might be able to help out on for a few days and bucks. He was supposed to meet up with his friend at lunch time to find out more.

Back at the marina, I told him, "Let me know how it goes with both the job and your folks."

"I will. Thanks again for coming out this morning."

He then surprised me with a tight hug.

"Sure. I enjoyed it," I said, wanting to melt into his arms.

He held me a beat longer than you would normally expect a friendly hug to last. I told myself he was just happy to have a friend.

Friend.

That was all we could realistically be.

I felt beat that afternoon after being in the bright morning sun and ended up taking a long nap in the luxury of the AC. When I woke up, I felt restless thinking about Troy. I couldn't believe how in a matter of a few days he had come to dominate all my thoughts.

I decided to head out to the Pub on Bourbon Street for a drink. The Quarter was a small place, and I usually ran into people I knew when I went out to any of the local watering holes. But when I got there, I didn't recognize anyone. Even the usual bartenders looked to be missing. Maybe everyone I knew went out of town for the holiday weekend. Everyone in the bar looked to be a tourist. The effect was odd and made me feel a little lonely and like a stranger in my own usual world.

I headed up to the second floor bar and found it mostly empty except for a few young twinky college aged guys standing in the corner and showing each other stuff on their cellphones. I headed out to the balcony and found myself alone now. I sat on a bench and watched small groups of tourists walk by below.

I found myself already missing Troy. Deep down I knew it was true. My teenaged crush had never gone away, and now it was turning into a full blown grown up infatuation. My heart already started to ache a little.

I could just break down, grow some balls, and tell him. But then I might lose a new friend. The guy already had so many things to deal with. We were in different places. And he was so…well, gorgeous.

But is there ever a perfect time?

Chapter Seventeen- Troy

My friend from high school, Barry, hired me to work with him a few days on a small remodeling and paint job he was doing in the Bywater. I was grateful for the work and the opportunity to do something different for a few days. And when I came out to Barry, since I figured I was on a roll, he appeared unfazed.

"Well, ain't that something," he said, chewing his tobacco and spitting the juice into a small empty Coke can. "Whatever makes you happy, buddy."

"That's all you have to say?" I asked, definitely expecting more.

"That's it," he said, shrugging. "That and you better do a damn good job for me on that house. I want to get word of mouth going to see if I can land work on any of those other houses in the Bywater that were just sold."

I was shocked at his non-reaction. I could only dream that it would be so easy with my parents.

The upcoming work would give me something to focus on in a couple of days which was good as I had no idea what the fallout from the "talk" with the parents would be.

I thought about Elliot and once again wished I could feel as comfortable and confident about who I was. There was something about him that made me feel...relaxed.

And then there was that kiss I drunkenly gave him. I wondered what he meant when he said he didn't mind it. Was he just trying to be nice? I also thought he didn't have an idea of how cute he really was. I realized he had the type of demeanor where I just wanted to put my arms around him, pull him close to me, and cuddle up next to him.

Why would he want a guy like me though? I was someone that hadn't even come out to his parents yet, and he was leading his life openly and proudly. I envied him for that, and I wondered if I would ever reach the same point.

"Is this really going to be it?" Louie asked me as we stared out of the kitchen window and looked at our father flipping burgers on the grill and our mother setting the picnic table.

"I'm going to do it. I can't put it off any longer, or it's going to drive me crazy."

Louie patted me on the back and said, "I'm here for you, bro. Whatever you need."

"Thanks," I said, swallowing hard. Butterflies went wild in my stomach as I looked at my father sternly tell my mother something about how she had set the table. It always had to be his way. *The only way.* My being gay would definitely not be the *right way* in his eyes.

"Can I ask you something a little off topic?" Louie said.

"Sure. Of course."

"What do you think of Elliot?"

"What do you mean exactly?" I asked.

"He's a good guy, right?"

"Right," I replied, wondering where this was going.

"I've always wished he could you know…find a good guy to settle down with. I think it's something that he wants, but he just seems scared to go for it."

"What are you getting at?"

"Well…" Louie said, his voice trailing off.

This couldn't be what I think it was. Would my brother actually be trying to play matchmaker? How surreal. Another thing I wasn't used to at all yet.

"I was thinking, you know? He's a good guy. You're a good guy."

"Are you trying to set me up with your friend?" I asked a little uncomfortable still talking about even the possibility of me having a love life with another guy.

"Just something to think about," he said, shrugging before breaking out into a sheepish grin and saying, "You know that is if Elliot's willing to take on a guy in this family."

"You're crazy," I said, shaking my head and not really providing my thoughts on the matter.

Our mother waved at us to come outside.

"Shit. This is it," I said. My palms started to sweat.

"It'll be okay. I'm with you all the way, bro."

I nodded truly grateful to have such a wonderful and supportive brother to stand by my side during this.

We walked out the backdoor, and our mom, in her high pitched voice, said, "What took y'all so long? What were you two talking about?"

"Nothing. Just talking," I said.

My mouth felt dry as cotton. I reached for a can of Pepsi, popped the top, and began to slug it down. Maybe some extra sugar and caffeine was all I needed for a little extra confidence.

"Well, the burgers are getting cold," dad said, placing the platter of patties on the table.

I started to tell him that there was no way the burgers were cold since he just took them off the grill seconds before, but I decided it would be best not to start this off in a confrontational manner.

Louie eagerly grabbed a bun and with the tongs picked a patty.

"I'm starved. These look great, Dad," Louie said in an unusual flattering tone with our father. Dad and Louie had never, and I mean never, saw eye to eye. I remembered that even when Louie was a toddler he managed to draw my dad into arguments about the silliest things.

Dad said nothing but started to build his own burger.

"This is just so…so…" Mom said, her eyes tearing up.

Oh, God. Not the waterworks. Not already. Mom teared up at dog food commercials. She always wore her emotions on her sleeve.

"I'm just so happy to have both of my boys home safe and sound. I worried and worried each and every day you were gone. You have no idea."

I had an exact idea. She was a worrier from way back. She practically dramatically passed out when I announced I was joining the service.

I just smiled and said, "It's good to be home."

"Any leads on a job yet?" Dad, forever focused on practicalities, said.

I looked at the platter of meat. I had no appetite. There was no way I could eat *now*.

"I'm gay," I blurted out loudly.

Louie, obviously not expecting the dramatic moment so soon, started to choke a little on his burger.

My father stared straight at the platter of patties avoiding eye contact. His face turned crimson from anger. I knew that look of his, the one he had right before he was going to blow up about something.

I glanced over at my mother, and she was frozen midway in putting pickles on her burger. She looked like all the blood had just drained from her face.

Dad loudly cleared his throat and said, "You'll need to get a job soon. You've been back for a while now, you know?"

I cut my eyes over at Louie who looked a little stunned at our father's response. He started to open his mouth to speak, but then shut it.

"Did you hear what I just told you, Dad?" I asked, perplexed.

"Unemployment's high now," he continued like I had never revealed anything. "You can't wait around because it might take extra-long to…"

"Dad, I said I'm gay," I repeated, this time louder.

Mom gasped a little and dropped her pickle on her plate. She too now stared at Dad waiting for some sort of response.

Dad cleared his throat yet again and reached for the bag of potato chips.

"Bobby Harper's boy came back from service and it took him six months to find something. Damned shame how we treat our veterans," he said, his face growing an even darker shade of red. He grabbed his beer bottle, took a swig, and slammed it back down. "Damned shame I tell ya."

I stood up. My breathing got heavier and my heart pounded. This is what he did when he didn't want to deal with an uncomfortable situation. He tried to ignore it. Damn anybody else, and my mother, who now looked at me with saucer wide eyes usually went along with him so as not to cause more "unpleasantness" as she called it.

Louie looked up at me on the edge of his seat waiting to see what I would do next. I must have looked a little lost because he said, "Mom, Dad, I think Troy's trying to tell you something important."

"Nobody asked you a damned thing," Dad snapped at him. "You're always living hand to mouth not having a steady job…"

"Fuck the job talk, Dad!" I blurted, surprising my own self. "You heard what I said."

I looked over at my Mom who had never looked so stunned in her whole life.

"You heard it, too, Mom. I'm not going to let you two sweep what I said under the rug and be in denial about what I just told you."

Dad looked up at me with a look of anger mixed with disgust.

"I don't want to hear this shit you're saying," he spat.

"Well, you're going to have to anyway," I said, standing my ground.

Dad looked taken aback. Louie and I had always tip-toed around him so as not to make him angry. But this time I wasn't going to let him get away with it. He was going to have to face my truth even if it meant letting me go as his son as a result. I had already been through a hard enough time not only living through a war but beating the battle that waged on inside me when it came to accepting me for who I was. I deserved the chance to lead my life openly after spending so many years living it in a way to make others feel more comfortable at the expense of my own soul.

"You watch what you say to me, boy," Dad said, his tone warning that at any second now his anger would explode.

"I'm not going to live a lie anymore whatever your opinion is of me. I spent the last few years of my life sacrificing for my country, and now it's time that I…"

Dad stood up suddenly and said, "You're disgracing your country and your family right now. I don't know what's gotten into your head, but one thing I know is that no son of mine is going to be a queer."

And with that he stormed back into the house, slamming the door behind him.

I looked over at Mom, and she appeared torn as to what to do.

"Are you going to say anything, Mom?" I asked quietly.

"Oh, Troy. I just…" her voice trailed off. "I think this is a lot for your father to take in."

"I'm not talking about him right now. I'm asking *you*!" I demanded.

She looked down into her lap and shook her head.

"This is just a lot all at once," she murmured.

She then stood up, too. She walked around to my side of the picnic table and placed a hand on my arm.

"Let me go check on your dad," she said, before heading into the house.

"Well, that went great," I said, looking down at Louie.

"Dude, you couldn't let me eat my burger first?" he said, chuckling.

I sat back down and took a deep breath.

"He hates me now," I said.

"Not true."

"Yes, it is. And Mom, well, she's not allowing herself to have an opinion at all."

"Give them time," Louie said softly.

"You know them as well as I do," I replied.

We both heard some yelling and door slamming coming from inside the house.

"I've got to go," I said, standing up. "I can't stay here any longer."

"Come on. I'll drive you back to my place. We'll have a beer then. Let these two have some time for it to sink in."

"Sink…in...right," I stammered.

Louie wrapped his burger up and placed it on a paper plate to take with him.

"Seriously, next time give me a heads up I should eat faster."

He smiled, and I knew he was doing his best to try and make me feel better. But we both knew the reality that was our parents. They would…or could…never change. Or at least I didn't believe it could happen.

Later that night, I sat on Louie's sofa staring at some bad reality shows on the TV while he went out to play a gig.

My mind was still spinning from the afternoon. Granted, I could have approached the subject with my parents better, but they still disappointed me. As much as I hated to admit it, there was a part of me that went into the situation wishing they might overcome any prejudices they may have had when I told them I was gay, give me a hug, and tell me it would all be okay. I knew that I had known better, but still I couldn't help but wish. I simply didn't know what to do next now.

My phone buzzed, and I checked it to find a text message from Elliot.

How did it go?

I wanted to pick up the phone and call him. I knew he'd understand, but I guess a part of me wasn't even ready to deal with what their reaction had been.

So, I texted back…

Kind of predictable. Can't really talk about it yet. Thanks for checking.

I hit the send button, and a wave of loneliness swept over me. I wanted to reach out. I really did, but sometimes when it came to the really emotional stuff I still didn't know how.

Chapter Eighteen- Elliot

Yikes! I knew it probably did go over like a lottery win with Troy's parents. Growing up, I was at his house enough to hear his parents, especially his dad, make some less than open-minded comments. But as I had learned, you never know how people would really react to hearing that their loved one is gay. Sometimes the ones you thought would be the least accepting are the most and vice versa.

Even though he said he didn't want to talk, I almost still called him, but then I stopped myself at the last second. Maybe he really didn't want to talk about it yet, and I should respect it. But there was a part of me that felt even more torn because I knew I wanted to comfort him…and as more than a friend.

The next morning, a Sunday, I was woken up by a special ringtone of Madonna's "Hung Up" and knew it was my cousin, Pat, calling me. The clock read eight o'clock. Pat was rarely up before eleven. So, I immediately sat up in bed and grabbed for the phone in case it was an emergency.

"What's up?" I asked hurriedly.

"*Goooood* morning," he said in his lazy drawl.

"Are you okay?"

"Well, I'm as fit as a fiddle thank you very much."

I sighed loudly and said, "You're never up this early."

"Well, I had to get up a little earlier because I hired someone to help me with the painting of the house and a few repairs. You know those manual laborer types like to get started early. Anyhow...I was wondering if you could...uh...bring by a few groceries I've been needing. I would go and get them myself, but that bad hip of mine is acting up. I just can't walk Poncho down to the store with me when my hip is like this."

For some odd reason, Pat insisted on taking Poncho with him when he went to the tiny little grocery store near his house. I always thought the idea of Pat walking with Poncho by the bacon section funny.

"Uh, sure," I said, realizing I might as well just get up now. "What do you need?"

"What?" he asked absentmindedly.

"At the store? What do you need me to get you?"

"Oh, yes! The store..." he said, his voice trailing off.

I could hear him quickly walking on his unbelievably creaky pine wood floor.

"You can get me..."

His honestly sounded like he had no idea what he actually wanted me to get him which was strange as he always knew exactly what was in his kitchen.

"Juice! That'd be good! And...hmmm...milk."

"Just juice and milk?" I asked, wondering if that really required a call so early. "Do you need to pick up any of your medicines at the pharmacy?"

"Oh, no. I'm completely stocked up on all my health pills...both the physical and mental ones," he answered, when I heard a muffled voice in the background. "Hold on a second. What did you say?" Muffled voice again. "Yes, start there *please*."

His voice hit a high tone that I knew was reserved for when he encountered a guy he thought was cute.

"I'm back. When you get here I might get you to help me...uh...hmmmm.....move some stuff, too."

"Sure," I said, wiping the sleep out of my eyes.

"Now you hurry over, okay?" and with that he hung up.

Hurry over?

Was his milk and juice situation that dire?

I threw back the covers, got out of bed, and stumbled towards the shower.

I knocked on Pat's door, and I immediately heard Poncho rooting and grunting on the other end of the door while some hammering went on in the back. I'm sure the neighbors loved the construction noises so early on a Sunday.

"I'm a coming!" I heard Pat scream out.

He opened the door, and I found him wearing a red kimono with his silver hair held back by a green hairband.

"Well, ain't you the sweetest?" he said, practically pulling me into the house. "Coffee's in the back. Come on!"

I held up the grocery bag with the milk and the juice and said, "Per your request."

He looked at the bag strangely for a moment and then said, "Oh, yes! That's right. Bring it to the kitchen."

The kitchen in the back of his shotgun was decked out in a rooster theme from rooster prints on the walls, to rooster placemats, to rooster salt and pepper shakers. If Pat could find it with a rooster on it, he bought it with the explanation, "I just love having a lot of cock around."

"That's a lot of hammering going on in the back," I commented.

I sat the grocery bag on the counter, and Pat immediately unloaded it and put the milk and juice in the fridge like an afterthought.

"Well, some things needed to be done, and I ain't as young as I used to be," he said.

"Anything I could have helped you with?" I asked, pouring myself a cup of coffee. This was a caffeine emergency if there ever was one.

Pat chuckled and said, "Honey, you're a great help to me with a lot of things, and I just love you for it. But let's be honest, you ain't exactly what somebody would call *handy with repairs.*"

It was true. I once tried to hang my own wallpaper to disastrous results.

"Point made," I replied.

"But you can go back out to the shed and bring in the…Christmas decorations."

"Pat, it's July," I said, stating what should be the obvious.

"Well…that's true, but I need to do inventory on it."

"Inventory on Christmas decorations in July?"

"Well, yeah," he said, hand on his hip. "It's all much cheaper in the off-season, you know. You can take your coffee with you. Oh, by the way…"

Oh, by the way…

I knew that sentence starter would mean what Pat really called me over for.

"There's a friend of yours out back," he said.

"A friend?" I asked quizzically.

"Yes. He saw you picture in the living room when he got here this morning. His eyes…well…they just lit up when they saw that snapshot of you. So, I thought it'd be great for you to come over…you know…while he's here…so you can say hello. That's right. Go say *hello.*"

He started to push me towards the backdoor, and I wondered who the hell he could be talking about. But before I could turn the knob on the door, Pat suddenly grabbed me.

"What's wrong now?"

"Oh, nothing. I just had to tell you that I think he's *to die for*," Pat said, before adding, "So don't fuck it up!"

I practically stumbled out the backdoor, my coffee spilling out of the mug, with Pat once again pushing me outside. I was stunned to come face-to-face with Troy wearing cargo shorts, a white tank top, and a tool belt.

"Troy?"

"Hey, Elliot," he said, smiling with a hammer in his hand.

Chapter Nineteen- Troy

That morning I couldn't believe the coincidence that the house my buddy had hired me to work on turned out to be Elliot's cousin that he had mentioned. As soon as I saw the framed picture of him and Elliot sitting on top of the television, I mentioned I knew him and we had been hanging out some lately.

His cousin's face had lit up, and he said, "Really? You don't say!"

And now just an hour later, Elliot was standing next to me in his cousin's backyard.

"Is this the house your friend hired you to help him remodel?" Elliot said, still looking surprised.

"Yep. What a coincidence, huh?"

"I'd say," Elliot said. Then some sort of look of understanding crossed over his face, and he looked back at Pat. "You didn't tell me my friend Troy was here."

"I wanted to surprise you," Pat answered through the screen door. He had a satisfied smug look on his face, and I now knew this for the early morning matchmaking event it really was. Then he held his hands up in the air and said, "*Surprise!* Now don't come back through here for a while cause I have to mop."

Then he slammed the door shut.

"Your cousin's a…character," I said.

"You don't have to tell me that," Elliot replied before adding a careful, "How are you doing after…well…you know?"

I shrugged my shoulders and said, "Well, it could've gone a little better than it did I suppose. But I can't say I was completely surprised."

"Sorry about that. How are you?"

"Okay. What can you do?"

Elliot nodded and looked a little lost about what to say next.

"Thanks for your text last night," I said. "It meant a lot to me. I just wasn't ready to talk about what happened."

"It's okay. I understand. But even if you ever just need to hang out with a friend, give me a call. We don't have to talk about what you don't feel like discussing."

"I appreciate that. I'm glad to have you as a…," my voice trailed off as I looked for the right words," friend right now."

"Anytime," Elliot said smiling.

I realized then how much his smile brought a sense of ease over me. With his grin and his boyish handsome looks, he really was a catch. I wondered why no one had grabbed him up yet.

"My cousin sent me out here to go get his Christmas decorations," he said, motioning to the shed in the back.

"Christmas in July?"

"Yeah, I don't really think that's why he called me over. He's always trying to play, well, to be honest, matchmaker. It's sweet. But sometimes it's a little embarrassing."

I laughed and said, "I thought maybe that's what it was from the way he was acting."

"God bless him. He has some roundabout ways of doing things, but he means well."

"I can tell he really cares about you. You're lucky to have him."

"I know," Elliot responded. He then looked at the back of the house and said, "So, what does he have you doing anyway?"

"Replacing the gutters and some of these boards are starting to rot," I said, pointing to some crumbling pieces of the house. "We'll put new ones on and then paint the whole house. A few days' work maybe. I'm grateful for it. I needed something to take my mind off of things."

"Well, you don't mind an audience for a little bit, do you?"

"Not at all. I think that's your cousin's plan anyway."

Elliot smiled again, but this time I noticed him blushing a little. He sat down on the back steps, took a sip of his coffee, and said, "I'm not exactly good with tools."

"Well, we all have our things we're best at," I said, pulling out some old nails from the boards to be replaced.

"I've always liked fixing things and being able to see the fruits of my labor."

"Ever thought about doing that for a living if it's something you enjoy?"

"Maybe," I answered. "I do need to figure out something here soon if just to keep myself out of trouble."

I winked at him, and realized before I knew it that I was indeed flirting.

"There are enough gay men in the area that would be happy to hire a hot guy for repairs, too," Elliot remarked before all of a sudden blushing again.

I knew then that he was flirting, too.

"Well, I don't know about all that, but thanks anyway."

"I only speak the truth," he said, trying to look innocent, and I couldn't help but grin.

I started to rip out some of the boards that needed replacing, and we spent a few minutes talking about the weather and how hot it already was when I finally blurted out, "It hurt like hell. Yesterday."

Verbalizing it to someone felt good. Like a little bit of pressure was being released.

"I know it must have," Elliot replied. "Sometimes people need…time. Especially when it comes to things they don't understand at first."

"I know," I said.

"But it still hurts," Elliot said, nodding knowingly.

"Yeah," I admitted. "It does. After always trying so hard to be…the perfect son…the idea that my being gay somehow wipes everything they've said they were proud of me for away."

Elliot stood up, walked over to me, and embraced me into a tight hug.

At first, I just stood there, but then I put my arms around him and hugged him back. It felt so good to have him in my arms. He pulled back a little and looked me in the eyes suddenly making me feel like I could melt right in front of him. We stood like that for a second and when I thought he was going to pull me into a kiss, he stepped back a little.

"Seriously, anytime you need to talk. I'm here for you, you know? I've been there," he said.

"I know. Thanks."

We stared at each other for another moment. It seemed like we were both waiting for the other one to make a move. And just when I was about to say to hell with it and bring him in for a deep kiss, this time not a drunken one, he stepped back a little more, smiled, and said jokingly, "I guess I better let you get some work done. I don't want to be a bad influence."

Feeling a little deflated, I said, "I guess I am on the clock," before I added hopefully, "Maybe you can hang out a bit though. You can tell me some more about what you've been up to while I was gone on duty."

"Sure," he said, walking back over to the steps and sitting back down. "Nothing too exciting though."

I focused my gaze on some more of the old nails I needed to pull out, took a deep breath, and said, "No special guys? There had to have been a special guy."

"Why do you say that?" Elliot asked, cocking an eyebrow.

I looked over at him and shrugged. "Because…I mean look at you."

"Look at me?" he said, laughing a little and blushing once again. "Why do you say that?"

"Well," I said, trying to sound a little more casual, while yanking out more nails. "You're smart. Cute. Caring. I can't believe there hasn't been a guy who's snapped you up yet."

He was quiet for a moment before he said, "I guess there's been a few close calls on that. A couple of boyfriends. But no one who, as Beyoncé would say, 'put a ring on it'."

I looked back at him and said, "Well, their loss then."

He smiled that heart melting grin again. He started to speak but stopped for a second. He appeared to be choosing his words carefully.

"Uh, I don't if you'd be interested, but my friend Joey is having a fundraiser tonight for his non-profit at a cabaret in Quarter. If you don't have anything else to do…"

"I have an extra ticket!" a voice shrieked from behind us as his cousin Pat almost fell through the screen door, obviously listening somehow to our whole conversation.

Both of us couldn't help but let out a chuckle as Pat almost stumbled on his way out the backdoor.

"Well, hello there," Elliot said, rolling his eyes but still smiling.

"I just happened to be coming outside when I heard y'all talking about the fundraiser," Pat said.

"Um, hmmm," Elliot murmured. "What a coincidence."

"Well, you know what a sucker I am for a cute face. So, when that hottie Joey caught me up at the Mardi Gras Zone on Royal. And we'll I couldn't help but buying a few tickets, and I just happen to have an *exxxxtra*. So, Troy here has no excuse," Pat said with a look of satisfaction on his face.

"Have anything going on tonight?" Elliot asked.

I shook my head. "Nah. I'm free. I'm just not sure I have anything to wear. Sounds like it might be a little formal maybe."

"Well, I'm sure that brother of yours has a suit you might be able to wear. You're definitely more...*muscular* though," Pat said, eyeing me up and down. "But I bet he still has something."

"Maybe. I'll ask and see what I can do," I agreed.

I had to admit to being a little nervous at the thought. I know. *Nervous.* After everything I've been through, but it would sort of be my first formal "gay" event.

"Well, I should let you get back to work if you're going to come to the fundraiser tonight," Elliot said to me before turning to Pat and adding dryly. "Unless you still need me to get those Christmas decorations, Pat."

"Oh, I think that can wait," Pat said before giving us a wink.

"Then I'll see you tonight?" Elliot asked.

"Sure. Let me see if that crazy brother of mine has something I can borrow."

"I have an idea!" Pat exclaimed. "Elliot, you should pick up Troy at his brother's so you know he doesn't get lost."

Elliot chuckled and his face flushed a bit before he said, "That…that sounds like a good idea. Okay with you? Pick you up at eight?"

"Okay. Sounds good," I said.

"Well, you run along now," Pat said, playfully slapping Elliot on the arm. "This man has work to do."

"See you later then," Elliot said.

"See you later," I said, watching Elliot and Pat head back inside.

I realized that tonight started sounding more and more like a date, and I wondered if I might get a chance to give Elliot a proper kiss.

Before he headed out to play another gig at a bar in the Marigny, Louie told me to wear anything I wanted from his closet. But I knew my brother had an eclectic sense of style to say the least. As I dug through his closet I found suits alright…ones that looked like a pimp would wear them. Finally, in the very back, I found a basic black suit. It wasn't the most exciting piece of clothing, but I figured with a nice tie it might do. Once I tried it on though, the pants were too baggy.

Shit!

After working the whole day, I certainly didn't have the time to go and buying something. And I couldn't wear my usual outfit of jeans and a white t-shirt for what sounded like a formal event.

Frustrated, I didn't know what to do, and then a knock on Louie's front door surprised me.

I headed into the living room, and when I opened the door I was taken aback to find my mother standing there.

"Mom!" I exclaimed.

I couldn't have been more shocked. We still hadn't spoken since the disastrous barbeque the day before.

"Hey," she replied. She looked a little nervous and was fidgeting with her purse. "I had to go do some shopping, and maybe I should have called. But I decided to take a chance."

"Uh, no problem. Come in," I said. I moved to the side and motioned for her to come inside.

She smiled and walked inside.

"I wasn't sure you'd want to see me," she admitted. "After yesterday."

"Why do you say that?"

"That I..." she stammered.

I knew she was having difficulty in knowing what to say as I did.

"I'm sorry, Mom," I said.

I felt myself starting to tear up, and I did my best to keep it inside. I couldn't even remember the last time I cried. But seeing my mother like this, so lost, and confused, I found myself flooded with guilt.

"Why are you sorry?" she asked.

"I could have...done yesterday a lot better," I said. "Sorry for that."

Mom took a deep breath, but she couldn't hold the tears in as they started flowing down her cheeks. She placed a hand on my cheek and said, "My sweet boy. Don't apologize. It was a little...surprising...but I know you did the best you could."

She walked over to the couch, sat down, and patted the space next to her for me to sit down which I did.

"I'm the one that should apologize," she said, shaking her head.

"Why?"

"I should've said more instead of running inside after your father like that. You know how he is when he gets upset or angry. And I did what I usually do. I run after him to make sure he's okay. But I should have stayed there with you and your brother and talked. That was the important thing. Will you forgive me?"

"There's nothing to forgive," I said. I reached over and took her hand in mine. "How's dad?"

"Not really speaking much. I won't lie to you. You know your father as well as I do. He's not good talking about feelings. Never has been. I tried to get him to talk but," she shrugged her shoulders, "He left early this morning to go fishing I think. I haven't seen him since."

"I'm not sure he'll ever understand," I said. "I know being gay is not what he ever imagined for one of his sons, especially me."

Mom chuckled. "It's true that if it had been Louie he probably would have just shook his head, muttered a few words, and that's it. Those two have never been able to see eye to eye on anything. But I think your dad saw you…"

"As the one like him," I finished for her.

She nodded and said, "Give him time."

"I don't know if he'll ever have enough time."

"I don't know, either, " she admitted. "But I'm glad you told us. I really am."

"You sure about that?"

"Definitely. I want you to feel that you can always be honest with me. I know sometimes I'm not the best with new things, either. But, you're my son. I'll always love you no matter what. And…"

"And what?"

"I kind of already had an idea."

"You did?" I said, beyond surprised. "I thought you'd be completely blindsided."

"Oh, honey. Parents often know more than what they let on. Call it instinct. I had an idea you may be gay, but I was too scared to bring it up. That's why I'm glad you did. So, we can finally get it out in the open."

"What clued you in?" I asked, still surprised.

"Well, you haven't really talked about or dated any girls since high school. And I remember your cousin Nancy's wedding."

"Nancy's wedding? What about that? I must have only been sixteen at the time."

"I just remember you standing on the side while everyone else was dancing in couples. You looked so lost and not in a shy wallflower way. But you just had the saddest look on your face like you didn't belong there. That was my first clue."

I couldn't believe she remembered that. I barely remembered anything from Nancy's wedding, and the fact that she picked up on something so subtle amazed me.

"Wow," was all I managed to say.

"I know it might take a while for things to readjust between us if you will. But I don't want you to ever feel like
that. Like you don't belong."

"What about Dad?"

She shook her head and said, "I don't know. I hope he
comes around. It just might take some time. Give him
some. You've had a while to deal with this. It's all new to
him. But no matter what I want you to know that I am
always here for you. Anything you need."

I wiped the tears out of my eyes. After feeling like the
situation with my parents was hopeless, I was filled a
renewed sense of the possibility that things may get better.
I reached out and gave her a big bear hug.

"I love you, Mom," I said.

"I love you, too, baby," she said, holding me tight.

When we pulled apart she surprised me again by asking, "Is there anyone special in your life?"

"Oh…"I choked out.

I was still getting used to the idea of being out to my
family. Discussing my love life felt like even deeper
territory.

"So, don't keep a mother waiting!" she said, chuckling.
"I want to know if a special guy has stolen my son's heart."

"Well…" I said hesitating. Should I tell her that Louie's friend, the guy she remembers as a little boy, had
managed to catch my eye, but I wasn't sure what would
happen yet. I decided to hold on to that nugget of infor-

mation longer to see how it played out. "There may be someone. But it's early. Too early to tell."

"Well, I hope it works out. You deserve to be happy."

"I was actually supposed to meet up with him to go to this charity event. But I don't have anything to wear. I looked to see if Louie had something to borrow, but…"

"Your brother's taste in clothes is sometimes questionable."

"Exactly. And the one black suit I found is too big in the pants. So, I don't know if I can go or not. I don't have much anything else, and it's too late to go shopping."

Suddenly, she stood up with a look of great purpose on her face.

"Where's this suit? I know Louie has a small sewing kit because I did alterations for him one time. I bet I can fix those pants in no time so that you're presentable."

"You think you can do that?" I asked.

"Never underestimate a mother's ability. Let's go look at that suit."

And for the first moment, I began to feel glad that I finally came out to my parents.

Chapter Twenty- Elliot

"Wow. You look amazing," I couldn't help but say when Troy opened the door.

He wore a suit that fit well in all the right places, and the tie he had on brought out the blue in his eyes.

"You clean up pretty good yourself," he said.

I had been a nervous wreck the whole afternoon getting ready trying to get just the right thing to wear. I was acting like a nervous schoolgirl going to her first dance and trying to catch the eye of the captain of the football team. But to me Troy was just like that. I never imagined that I would ever even get to spend this much time with him. He had always been that crush that you lust after from afar but never expect anything to come of it. Now, a little part of me was beginning to wonder if there was a chance. The problem was if there was a possibility of something happening I didn't know if I trusted myself to go for it. The same thoughts haunted me. He's so gorgeous. He's out of your league. He just came out. He'll need time to experiment and sow his wild oats.

In other words if something did happen, I just feared he would break my heart, and I knew with him that heartbreak would be especially tough.

My *risk management* training from work had a hold over me that was very hard to ignore.

Yet, here I was. Well, thanks to Pat's not so subtle matchmaking I was spending more time with Troy in a situation that well…sort of…felt like a date.

"Are you ready to experience the craziness that is Belinda's at Savannah's?" I asked.

"I think so," he said.

He looked a little nervous which made me realize maybe I wasn't the only one with butterflies this evening. Were they for me or just attending this huge gay fundraiser?

As we walked down Dauphine and headed down to the cabaret I filled him in on some of the background of the place such as how my friend Mason's aunt used to own it before she passed away and how from what I hear she used to be the mom figure to the whole gay community in the Quarter. Mason and Joey ran it for a few years before selling it to both Miss Althea, the most famous drag queen in New Orleans, and Belinda, a local famous restaurant owner. The place was still known for outlandish drag shows and now some of the best Creole cooking in the city. It had remained a gay and lesbian landmark in the city and fundraisers were often held there.

"How did you meet Mason and Joey?" he asked as we neared the cabaret.

"I had just moved back to town after going to LSU, and I met them at one of these fundraisers actually. I was looking for a way to get involved in the community and Joey put me right to work. Once I got to know them, I don't know…it was…it was great getting to know a gay couple that just seemed to fit together so well. I guess it gave me hope."

We stopped right outside the cabaret and got in line behind a few people who were waiting to pay their cover charge.

"So, is that what you want one day?" he asked. "Someone to *fit* with?"

"I guess you could say that. Yes," I answered.

I so badly wanted to tell him I wanted to fit with *him*.

"I thought about what you said, too," Troy said.

"About?"

"Going into business for myself. I mentioned it to the friend I'm working for, and he says he could use a partner he has so much work lately."

"That's excellent!" I enthused. "You'll be great."

"I guess I really am back home for a while," he said, with a grin.

I thought about Leslie's job lead for me in Houston. Just when I thought I was maybe ready to leave New Orleans and get a fresh start somewhere new…and now this…whatever it was with Troy was happening.

Timing for things in my life always seemed to be off.

When we walked into the lobby of the cabaret everything was packed wall to wall with people.

"Wow. Looks popular," Troy commented.

"I'm glad to see so many people out for a good cause.
It's like the whole local gay community is here. Want
something to drink?"

"Just a beer for now would be good."

But before I could make my way through the crowd to
the bar I heard Joey yell out, "'Bout time you made it!"

Both Joey and Mason, wearing tuxes, walked over to
us.

"Everything looks great," I commented.

The lobby had been decked out with tiny white lights
hanging from above and bouquets of multi-colored roses.

"Thanks in a big part to you," Joey said. "The florist
contact you had did an amazing job. Wait until you see the
main floor and all those silent auction items you found for
us."

"Wait until you see the *show*," Mason said. "Miss Althea did a bang-up job with the line-up. I saw the rehearsal
this afternoon."

They were both talking to me, but their eyes were on
Troy. I knew they were scoping him out and trying to
figure out if this was my mystery man.

"I'm Mason, and this is my partner, Joey," Mason said
holding out his hand to shaken.

"Troy," Troy said, shaking both of their hands.

"Nice to meet you, Troy," Joey said.

Mason and Joey both cut their eyes over at me and gave me a big grin. Obviously they approved. Who wouldn't though? Troy had never looked more dashing as he did that evening.

"We've heard *a lot* about you," Mason said.

They had? I'd barely talked about him.

"Hey, babies!" I heard Pat call out as he made his way over to us, too.

So *that's* where they heard a lot from.

Pat, wearing a light baby blue suit and yellow tie, walked over looking very pleased with himself at seeing me with Troy.

"Glad to see both of you made it," Pat said.

"Thanks again for the ticket. I appreciate it," Troy said.

"Anytime, honey," Pat said. He took a sip of wine before he said, "Don't the two of you just look so *cute* together."

I felt myself blush deeply. Damn it. I could never hide my embarrassment. Troy and I hadn't even had a conversation about rather this was a real date or just two friends spending an evening together.

Joey turned to Troy and said, "Elliot here is responsible for a lot of the success tonight."

"Really?" Troy said in surprise before turning to me and saying, "You never mentioned that."

"It was no big deal," I said shrugging my shoulders. "I love doing it."

"Trust me it's a big deal," Joey insisted. "In fact, the board approved the hiring of a full-time fundraiser. I'd hire Elliot here in a second."

"Impressive," Troy said, smiling.

I wondered if Joey were serious about the fundraiser job. Wow. I bet I'd have a blast if that's what I spent my work day doing. But I couldn't just leave my actuary job, could I? I'd worked so hard just to get to this point. To make such a dramatic career change would be…impractical.

"If you'll excuse us both we need to check on some things," Joey said, taking Mason's hand.

"Of course," I replied.

"And I'm going to leave you two alone so you can have a chance to *talk*," Pat said, raising both of his eyebrows and heading off in the direction of some people he knew.

"Well, what about that beer after all?" I asked.

"Sounds good," Troy answered.

"Be right back," I said, heading over to the bar to place my order.

While I waited for the drinks I watched Troy as he looked over some of the New Orleans themed paintings on the wall…a jazz band, a balcony scene, Jackson Square, and Armstrong Park. He looked a little nervous, unsure of himself here which was kind of endearing. One thing for sure was that *everyone* was checking him out from the corner of their eye. New Orleans may be a city, but it can often feel like a small town in certain circles. No doubt people were wondering who the new handsome guy in town could be. I'll admit; it was a little intimidating to be out with a date…I mean *friend*…who garnered so much attention. I didn't know whether to be flattered that he was here with me tonight or jealous.

Screw it. It's time to be bold. Roll the dice and see what happens.

I was so freaking tired of second guessing myself and of running statistics and risk reports in my head about everything. To be honest, I was damned tired of being afraid. Afraid of taking a chance on something, anything, in my personal life.

I inhaled a sharp breath to work up my nerve and walked back over to Troy. I handed him the drink and said, "Want to head upstairs and see what's part of the silent auction?"

"Sounds good," he answered.

And then in a very un-Elliot move, I took his free hand in mine and led him upstairs. As we walked up the steps, I felt him lightly squeeze my hand. I turned back to look at him and he smiled.

After we looked over the silent auction items I had secured donation to, pieces of art, gift certificates to restaurants, and such, I realized that I really did make a huge contribution to the evening. I wondered why I could never give myself credit for the things I did and why I always had to downplay any success.

We eventually made our way outside to the second floor balcony and took in the cooler evening air...still holding hands. A few other attendees socialized in small groups, and we made our way over to an empty table and set down our drinks.

"Did I already tell you how amazing you look tonight?" I asked.

Troy beamed and said, "Thank you. And thank my mom."

"Your mom?"

"She came over to Louie's after I got off from work to talk to me."

"She did? What did she say?"

"I think things are going to be okay with her. My dad...hmmm...I don't know yet."

"It's still early," I pointed out. "You're dad's old school in his beliefs, but that doesn't mean he won't come around one day."

"That's what I'm hoping. Anyway, the suit didn't fit, and she did some last minute alterations. And here I am!"

he said, stepping back and posing with a goofy grin on his face.

"Your mom does great work," I said. "And I'm glad she talked to you. I know it meant a lot to you."

"It did. I'm glad I came out to them. Sure, I could have done it a little better maybe, but what's done is done. The important thing is that I did it."

"I agree. I'm very happy for you," I said.

And then I surprised myself with another bold move. I put my arms around him and pulled him in tight for a hug, and he responded with the same. When we pulled back, our eyes met, and then right when we started to move in for a kiss, Mason came out on the balcony through one of the doors and called out, "Everyone, the show's starting soon if you'd like to make your way back downstairs."

We both chuckled. Another almost kiss thrown off course.

"I guess we better head downstairs then," he said. "I've never seen one of these drag shows before."

"You haven't?" I said in surprise.

"Never," he said, shaking his head. "Kind of curious to see what one looks like."

"Well, you certainly won't forget it anytime soon…at least not one of the shows here," I replied, taking his hand again. "Let's go!"

We watched all of the performers including the opening number with Miss Althea in a blonde wig doing Lady

GaGa's "Poker Face" while accompanied by worked out young college aged guys, each wearing a different colored speedo, dancing around her as soap suds fell from the ceiling. I don't know how they managed that one. She was followed by other drag performers such as Miss Hurrie Kane, Miss Diana Boss, and Cherry Bomb all performing to such classics as "I'm Coming Out" to recent hits from Rhiana. Each performance had a meticulously choreographed number with cute young guys as back up dancers.

Troy didn't seem to know exactly what to make of it all, but he laughed at all the right comical bits and appeared to be enjoying himself.

In total, the night proved to be a big success as Joey announced on the stage that they had raised $25,000 through the course of the evening.

As the crowd began to thin out and the night grew long, I began to grow a little nervous. Should I just walk him back to Louie's like a good little gentleman and bid him adieu for the night? I didn't know if I felt comfortable…uh…hanging out there with Louie, my childhood friend, returning at any moment. Not that Louie would probably give a rat's ass, but it still felt a little odd to me.

A panic began to sweep over me as I suddenly didn't know how to end the evening on the right note, but then I was saved when Troy said to me, "Maybe we should head back to your place and…talk some more. If you're up for it."

"Oh, I'm up for it," I said, before blushing at what "up for it" could imply.

Chapter Twenty-One- Troy

Okay. I gotta admit I was a little nervous, but I was proud of myself for being so bold as to suggest that we go back to Elliot's. For a second, I hoped that I didn't push too far too fast or suggest something that maybe he wasn't ready for, but when his eyes lit up at the suggestion, I knew I was on the right track.

As we walked back to his place, there were moments of shyness that popped up as if we both were teenagers on their first date again. Hell, for me it kind of was my first real official date. I had dated girls in high school, but I never felt nervous about it really for obvious reasons except when I thought the girl might be expecting more than I wanted to give. Don't get me wrong, I tried. I tried to kiss, to cuddle, to screw the gay away with some females, but it never felt right or even the least bit fulfilling.

Now, this was a different ball game, so to speak.

"I'm glad I got to go with you tonight to that fundraiser," I said, as we started walking down the less congested and residential streets of the Quarter. The full moon provided most of our light. "It sort of gave me a lot of hope."

"Hope in what way?" Elliot asked.

"Meeting your friends, feeling that sense of community. It showed me what finally being out could really mean. Holding your hand as we walked around was nice, too."

I reached out and took his hand into mine as we stopped in front of his building. I couldn't wait any longer. I reached out and pulled him into me and kissed him deep and passionately right there on the street. His body felt warm against mine and his lips soft.

We stood there for a few good minutes kissing deeper and deeper, the clothes we had on between us feeling like an unwelcome barrier.

"Maybe we should head on up," Elliot said, a little breathless.

"Yeah, that might be a good idea," I replied. Especially before I was tempted to tear off his clothes right then and there.

I had had my share of sexual encounters with other guys the past few years. Someone I met in out and about. Another soldier that held my stare just a beat longer than a straight one ever would. But that's all they had been really was encounters. This was the first time I felt heart tugging emotions behind every touch and not just unbridled lust. Sure, I had carnal urgings where Elliot was concerned. His boyish good looks and lack of awareness of just how cute he was proved to be a huge turn on to me. But the fact that I genuinely cared for him and wanted to get to know more about him added a whole new dimension for me when it came to the physical.

Once we were inside and had caught our breaths, he asked, "Would you like something to drink?"

I thought about going along with the pleasantries and maybe asking for some water or another beer. But then I decided, screw it! I knew what I wanted, and it sure as hell wasn't coming in a glass.

"All I want right now is you," I said, pulling him into my arms again and kissing his mouth and then his neck as my fingers trailed down from his throat, over his chest, down past his belly, and then to below the belt.

"Troy, you have no idea how much I've always wanted to do this with you. This is like a teenage fantasy come true all these years later. I would have never dreamed that it might actually come true."

"You're such a sweet guy," I said. "And I want you to know I truly like you, want to keep getting to know you, and you aren't the only one with a crush."

"Really?" Elliot said, his eyes widening.

"*Really*," I said.

I threw off my jacket and tie and let them hit the floor as did he. I pulled him back next to me and admitted, "I want to stay here for the night with you. I want to make *you* feel good."

"Damn, you have no idea how good that sounds," Elliot said in a half-whisper.

I took his hand and led us back to his bedroom where I told him, "I don't think I can wait much longer. Undress for me."

He swallowed hard and then slowly began to unbutton his shirt, then his belt, and unzipped his pants. His pants hit the floor, and I couldn't help but chuckle a little when I saw the Superman boxer shorts he wore.

"Yeah, it's not the sexiest underwear. I didn't think I'd be lucky enough for this to happen," he said sheepishly.

"I think it's cute," I said. "And it looks like Superman's ready to take flight down there, too."

He laughed nervously, and I started to take off my clothes until we were both standing there only wearing our underwear, me in my white boxer briefs, my manhood straining against the cotton fabric.

"Like I said, I want to make you feel good, like you deserve to have a man make love to you," I said, pulling him against me again.

Now as the skin on skin contact increased so did the excitement for both of us. The heat between our two bodies intensified as I laid him down on the bed.

"For so long, I wanted to feel this way with another guy," I croaked out. "I feel lucky it's with you."

"Nah, I think I'm the lucky one," Elliot said, reaching out and pulling me down on top of him and into another hungry kiss.

Epilogue- Elliot

Professional that quantifies risk.

So, now I'm lying on the bed next to Troy watching him sleeping peacefully after we made love. Just watching him breathing softly, his muscular chest slowly rising and falling, was heaven. And I can actually say that. *Made love.* What just happened was not simply having sex, but a feeling of being so connected that the whole experience took on a spiritual quality.

Yeah. I don't think I can deny it any longer. I'm falling, and it goes so against all my professional training. I shouldn't be doing this, my actuary brain tells me. You're falling too fast and deeply with a man who still has so much to work through. The risk you're taking could get you hurt.

To hell with it! To hell with always being too scared to take any personal risks. To hell with watching other people couple up and have what I've always wanted. To hell with fear.

I also found myself seriously considering Joey's job offer. Who says it's ever too late to reinvent yourself?

I don't know how it will all turn out in the end, but I now know one thing. I won't have to wonder. I'm over wondering "what ifs." From now on, I'm going to *do* because what I just felt was so much better than what my fear of being hurt ever led me to.

I wrapped my arms around Troy and pulled him closer to me, took in his intoxicating scent, and felt his heartbeat next to my hand.

About the Author

Also by Michael Holloway Perronne:
A Time Before Me
Falling Into Me
A Time Before US
Starstruck: A Hollywood Saga
Embrace the Rain

www.michaelhperronne.com

www.ingramcontent.com/pod-product-compliance
Lightning Source LLC
Chambersburg PA
CBHW060620130626
46555CB00002B/581